A Midwinter
Night's Dream

# A Midwinter Night's Dream

Jimmy Brokaw

A Midwinter Night's Dream
copyright James Brokaw 2015

Published by Hedgie Press
First printing February, 2015

**ISBN-13: 978-0984702169**
**ISBN-10: 0984702164**

Cover art by Melody Daggerhart
Hedgie Press logo by Amanda Ulevich

*This book is dedicated to Andrea Brokaw, my loving wife, without whom this book would not exist.*

*As a teenager, she gave me my love of Shakespeare. In our twenties, she helped encourage me to apply my love of skiing and turn it into a career.*

*And now, in my thirties, she did all the hard work to turn a text file on a computer into a book. Through our twenty years together, she has made my life nothing less than a dream.*

*Pereant, inquit, qui ante nos nostra dixerunt*

-Aelius Donatus

# 10:30 PM

# Resort President's Office

There are few things prettier than the sound of falling snow. The sound of snow is a mesmerizing, wonderful music that can bring to mind to the most glorious of days or the most romantic of nights. Every snowfall sounds different; the strength of the snow crystals, the force with which they hit the ground, even the humidity of the air can change the quiet music of snowfall into a million different melodies. It is a truism that all children know that snow is magical, but only a lucky few remember this into adulthood.

Tonight's snowfall was harsh. Strong winds brought the snow down brutally, but it didn't just pile up there. The gale-like air served its role as nature's bulldozer, picking it back up and swirling it around, pushing and shoving it, and making deep piles wherever it chose to eddy. The fragile arms would break off the flakes, leaving small crystals and fragments densely packed together. To our winter musician, it left high notes easily lost in the howling of the wind. To the forest ranger patrolling the backcountry, it meant a high avalanche danger and the possibility of search and rescue come morning. To Theo and Lita Rigas, however, it meant a solid base layer – and that meant money.

Theo was the president of Ridge Mountain Ski Resort, and it had not been a good year so far. Warm days and dry nights had conspired to keep the base shallow, which led to fewer skiers and fewer profits. Theo wasn't really worried, however. It was a La Niña year, and La Niña frequently gave the Northwest a mild early winter with a hell of a bang at the end. Early season profits might be below average, but the overall year was bound to recover. This storm was the first sign of life for what otherwise would have been a failed winter for the small ski resort, and it was coming late enough that everyone had been nervous.

"Look at it coming down!" Lita grinned as she looked out the window, her expression changing to make her appear decades younger. "We really need this snow, but do you think we can get it groomed and open by morning?"

"It's supposed to taper off around three. The groomers will have no trouble getting it into shape by the time the lifts start turning." Her husband looked out the window at the tempest. "Might even get the pipe carved for tomorrow."

"That would be great. God, I thought we would be hosting a snow festival without snow!" The

Ridge Mountain Snow Festival was the largest event the mountain ran each year, drawing the crowds up from Seattle and Portland and into the mountains. Even those who didn't ski or snowboard would come to watch competitions, drink beer, and listen to rock bands from around the country.

"Speaking of, is everything good to go?" Theo had placed his wife in charge of the Snow Festival many years ago, and under her charge it had grown almost as large as the resort itself. There was never any question she was the right woman for the job.

"It's going well, actually. Have you seen the musical lineup? The Angry Sex Puppies are headlining tomorrow night. The Puppies will be a big draw; they've got a number one song out right now."

"Really? I've never heard of them. What's the song?"

"*Tripping on the Nosegays*. It's pretty catchy."

"Lita, for the life of me, I have no earthly idea what a nosegay is."

Lita laughed. Both Rigases were now in their sixties, but Lita had retained a better understanding of youth than her husband. "Don't worry, I've got the usual bluegrass bands playing Sunday morning on the second stage. Remember, it's all about bringing folks up the mountain to see what we have to offer here."

"I know, Lita, I know." Theo looked back out the window. "Are you ready to go yet? We'll take the sled home tonight."

"Sure, just let me log off here." Lita saved her work and was waiting for her applications to close when there was a rap on the door. "Who could that be?"

"Come in!" shouted Theo, curious as to who was still at work in the office at this late hour.

George Markos, Ski School Director, popped his head in the door. "Got a sec?"

Theo nodded affirmatively.

"Thanks, appreciate it." George sat down in the leather coach positioned against the side wall underneath an oversized canvas print of the main base area. "I just wanted to talk to you about a personal issue that's got me vexed."

"Oh, do you need some privacy?" asked Lita.

"Oh, no, nothing that personal. Just an issue with Mia." Mia was George's daughter, and she had been a ski instructor at the mountain for the last four winters.

Theo sagely nodded again. Without a word, he reached down to his bottom drawer and pulled out a bottle of Jack Daniels along with two shot glasses. "Will this help?"

"Indubitably." The pair drank the whiskey down quickly, and George began his tale. "Mia's dating Alex now.... Do you know Alex?"

"No, I don't think I do. What does he look

4

like?"

"He's a rookie ski instructor, wet behind the ears and tongue frozen to the lift tower. He's a kid, and it shows. I mean, he can ski just fine, but he's got no drive, no ambition, and he barely understands the teaching model. It's not that he's done anything wrong, but I don't see a future for the kid."

"Wait a second," interrupted Lita. "I thought Mia was dating Demetri?"

"They dated for a while, but she broke it off! Can you believe it?" George looked at Theo and Lita to see if they could, but failed to interpret the blank expressions. "Anyway, Demetri is pretty upset about it, and to be honest, so am I. Demetri is a rising star, consistently leading the hours for instructors, and on the fast track to management in the resort. Why would she leave him for a loser?" Theo and Lita could only shrug in response, so George continued.

"So Demetri comes to me earlier this week, and says he wants to marry Mia. Not just date her again, but marry her! This is wonderful news to me; I couldn't think of a better man for her. Of course I tell him he's got my blessing, but he would have to give me some time to talk her into it. That's when I found out she was dating this louse Alex."

"Last night I was so angry, I told Mia she had to dump Alex and marry Demetri or I'd cut her off completely."

"You what?" interjected Lita.

5

"I told her I'd cut her off. Fire her from the school and stop giving her money and a place to live. She turned eighteen; I don't have to support her anymore!" George's Greek accent was getting stronger, as it always did when his temper was riled.

"Yes, exactly, she's eighteen. She can date whomever she damn well pleases, I should think!"

"Alright, Lita," interrupted Theo. "Let George finish his story."

"Well, that's really the long and short of it. Mia's pissed off at me, but if she doesn't make the right choice, I swear to God she'll be out on the street before the snow melts."

Theo turned his empty shot glass in his bony fingers. George was fifteen years his younger, but he was Theo's best friend at the resort, and they served as each other's personal confidants. "Tell you what, George. I can't say I think you're doing the right thing, but she's your daughter, not mine. It's a wise man who understands his daughter, and I'll give you the benefit of the doubt on that one. What can I do to help?"

"Theo!" interjected Lita.

"I'd like your permission to fire both Mia and Alex should she refuse my offer, that's all."

"George!" interjected Lita.

"George, you've never needed my permission to hire and fire as you see fit within the Ski School, you know that."

"Yes, but I'd like your explicit permission. After all, this is my daughter we're talking about."

"Consider it granted, then. Another round?" Theo lifted the bottle an inch off the table.

Lita grabbed the snowmobile keys from the desk. "Drink all you want. I hope you find another way home, I'm leaving." She briskly stomped out of the office, slamming the door behind her as she left.

"What do you suppose that was all about?" asked Theo as the sled roared to life outside.

# 6:30 AM

## Lift Attendant Locker Room

It is difficult to describe the job of lift attendant so that it sounds attractive. Lift attendants must arrive early, well before the resort opens. They must spend long hours outside, in inclement weather. They must be prepared to do exhaustive physical labor. They must deal with frustrated patrons and squirming children. If they allow their attention to waver for even a second, someone could be seriously injured. They often earn minimum wage, or close to it, yet they do it with a smile.

When asked why they take this low paying difficult job, a lift attendant will look back at you incredulously. "I work outside, at a ski resort. I spend all day on the side of a mountain! You spend all day inside a cubicle, in an office. The real question is, why do *you* do it?"

And they're absolutely right.

Lifties, as they are alternately known both affectionately and derisively, are not morning people. However they are the first to the mountain after the groomers, who work through the night. The lifts pull skiers up, and gravity pulls them down, in an endless cycle of pleasure. Without the lifts, the mountain comes to a standstill. Before noon, the romance of the idea is invariably lost on lifties, who instead curse the mother of whoever brewed the latest batch of never-strong-enough coffee. This morning the lift attendants sat gathered around the table, sipping hot coffee out of insulated mugs.

Peter rapped his pen on the table with a light clink. "Alright, let's get this thing started." Peter was the supervisor of the lift attendants, mostly by virtue of longevity. Longevity, in this case, turned out to be a polite way of saying stubbornness, and perhaps even pig-headedness. "We'll go through the roster to ensure we're all here. Nick?"

"Fuck you," responded Nick.

Peter did not take the bait from Nick. "Frank?"

"Peter, you can see us all," replied Frank. "We're all here. Get on with it."

"Get on with it!" replied the lifties, in unison, the product of too many nights watching *Monty Python and the Quest for the Holy Grail* under the influence of alcohol and stronger agents.

Peter glared at the men gathered around the

tables. He felt they intentionally made his job difficult. "Alright, fine, we won't do a muster. But if anyone isn't here and I mark them as present, then someone's going to have some explaining to do!"

Peter settled into his rehearsed speech. Each morning he went through the morning meeting inside his head, but what came out rarely resembled what he had envisioned. "Okay, I don't need to say this twice – it's the Snow Festival, and the biggest weekend of the year for us. Everything I've been talking about all year goes double today. Be polite to the guests." There was a distinct pause and a directed stare at Stan right after the *polite to guests* reminder. Stan had narrowly avoided termination for a recent incident in which he had rather aggressively confronted a teenager who had cut the line. As it turned out, the teen was mentally disabled and participating in a special needs program, but had managed to get free from his group for some authorized and unsupervised free skiing. "No smoking in uniform, be on time for shift changes,"

"Look, Peter, the snow's real deep out there," Tom broke in. "It's gonna take us a long time to dig out the lifts – can we skip the BS talk this morning and get cracking on the real work?" It was obvious the coffee was too weak this morning, and everyone's nerves were thin.

Peter looked down at the yellow sticky note he had spent twenty minutes crafting, detailing all the reminders he was to give to the crew, along with an inspirational quote to motivate them. He had gotten the bottom of the sticky note wet coming into the building, and now the inspirational quote was smeared beyond recognition. He sighed, crumpled the note, and stuffed it into his pocket.

"Alright, fine. But we need to talk about our skit for the festival tonight." There was a round of groans. "We'll be performing tomorrow morning, so I've printed out lines. We'll be doing the balcony scene from *Romeo and Juliet* this year!" There was another round of groans. "Frank, you'll be Romeo."

Frank took the sheet from Peter. "Forsooth, I shall merrily away to estudy my lines, verily and muchsuch."

"And Nick, you'll be playing Juliet." Peter handed Nick his lines.

"But Juliet is a girl! I can't play Juliet!"

"Why not? In Shakespeare's day all the actors were men!"

"Yes, but I've got a mustache! Get Tom to play Juliet, he's practically a girl anyway." The entire group looked over at Tom, but it appeared the coffee wasn't strong enough to keep him awake, and no retort was forthcoming.

"Look, you're playing Juliet and that's final. It's supposed to be funny anyway, so the mustache just

11

going to make them laugh more."

Frank choked on his coffee. "Funny? *Romeo and Juliet* is a tragedy! We shall make this the saddest skit of the year, and there won't be a dry eye in the house tonight."

"What about me?" inquired Robin. "I wanted to be in the skit this year, remember?"

Peter hesitated, thinking quickly. "You can play the part of..." He mentally recited the entire scene in his head, as best he could. "The moon! You'll be the moon!"

"The moon doesn't have any lines. I want a speaking part."

"Well, then..." Peter thought again. "You can play the part of Romeo's faithful dog!"

"The dog doesn't have speaking lines, either." Robin did not appear pleased with Peter's creative interpretation of the bard's work.

"Sure it does, it goes 'Woof!'"

"No, I want a speaking part."

"Okay, okay," said the exasperated manager. "You can be Romeo's talking dog. Just adlib a few lines in to agree with Romeo, and console him when he's upset. Piece of cake."

Robin leaned back in his seat, basking in the rare victory over the unyielding policies of upper management. He had earned himself a speaking part in the skit to be performed at the Snow Festival.

"Alright guys, time to start digging out. Those of you with speaking parts read over them and practice on your breaks. Everyone else, come back here to help build the set pieces as soon as you get off the lifts. Lift assignments are on the board. Now get out of here!"

# 7:30 AM
# Snow Sports School
# Locker Room

In the movies, locker rooms are large areas where each instructor has his own locker, large enough to store his gear. They resemble high school locker rooms except with neon beer signs hanging from the walls, and fewer half-naked teenagers. These locker rooms do not exist outside of Hollywood. Nor do ski school locker rooms resemble the clean rooms designated as public changing areas, where you can store your shoes in a locker the size of a breadbox for only five dollars a day.

Real estate on a mountain is expensive, and resorts must dedicate as little as possible to areas that cannot be used by the general public. As a result, ski school locker rooms are in the most undesirable areas, tucked away in attics and basements, far from the public eye. They are small and cramped, never large enough for the actual staff. Lockers are not provided for all instructors; only the top ranked instructors are permitted to keep gear locked up overnight, while everyone else must carry all their equipment to and from the mountain each day.

The floors are invariably carpeted to reduce damage to ski boots. Each instructor walking in brings clumps of snow, which melt and soak the padding. The carpet remains wet all winter long and degrades quickly.

Heating is always an issue. If the locker room is kept too warm, it causes a shock to the system when going outside to teach. If it's kept too cold, frozen instructors needing to warm up will do so in public areas, displacing paying guests. The best compromise happens to be one of the more cost-effective ones – the room is kept cold with a high-powered space heater in one corner for the huddling masses.

In short, ski school locker rooms are not nice places.

Like most locker rooms, the Ridge Mountain Snow Sports School locker room was built to hold half the instructors that currently worked at the resort. Lockers were narrow and thin, and the doors swung open almost to the bench that ran down the middle of each aisle. When the room was full, one required a certain amount of nimbleness simply to navigate from one end to the other; a trait fortunately shared by the majority of instructors. Unfortunately, the athletic odors of the locker room did not share the nimbleness, and instead lounged around lazily, wafting into every nostril in the room.

Alex opened the door and entered the locker room, bringing a miniature avalanche of snow inside with him. He hadn't taken three steps inside before hearing a cacophony of voices screaming in unison, "Shut the door!" It wasn't particularly cold outside this morning, but it was far colder than it had been so far this winter. Three feet of fresh powder did a lot to put the instructors in a good mood, but an open door was an open door, especially when you were standing around in thin socks.

Alex spied one of his friends as he opened his locker to retrieve his gear. "Yo, Demetri." Demetri was already suited up and ready for the morning meeting; he was idly reviewing his lesson plans for his regular Saturday children's group.

"Hey, Alex. Great snow out there today. Hope I don't lose any kids in the pow." His cheerful countenance was shared by everyone in the room; fresh snow will do that to ski instructors.

Alex laughed. "Oh, better to suffer from too much pow than sticks and stones poking through the snow!"

Demetri agreed with a silent nod.

"Hey, Alex!" chirped Mia, walking through

the group on her way to her locker. She gave him a quick peck on the cheek, oblivious to the expression on Demetri's face. "Great snow! I gotta get my boots on, but I'll catch you later, 'kay?" She moved down the aisle, leaving as suddenly as she had arrived.

Mia's brief presence had warmed the air momentarily, but in her absence it was notably chillier than before. Alex saw the scowl on Demetri's face and, in a rare moment for him, recognized it. "Hey man, don't be like that."

"Be like what? You really think she's going to move with you to your uncle's farm in Idaho when the season ends? No, she'll stay right here, and you'll have done nothing but waste her time."

"Oh, fuck off, Demetri. You're just full of sour grapes, no need to ruin everyone else's happiness."

"I'm not ruining anyone's happiness. In fact, I'm as happy as a penguin in a fish factory." The veracity of the latter statement was tempered by the growl with which he spoke.

"Not that it matters," Alex replied, "but you haven't exactly been fair with the ladies yourself."

Demetri stood up. "And just what the hell is that supposed to mean?"

"Come on, Demetri, what about you and Helen…? You're taking advantage of her just because she's got a crush on you."

"What are you talking about?"

17

"You sleeping with Helen, then breaking her heart. You really shouldn't take advantage of a girl like that; leading her on just to get her in the sack."

"What? I never… Helen and I never… Who's spreading this rumor?"

"Whatever, Demetri," Alex averred. "Everyone knows."

At the far end of the same aisle, Mia was waggling the tongue of her boot to squeeze her foot in, whilst waggling her own tongue with Helen. "So, what's this rumor about you and Demetri hooking up at the Double Black last night?" The Double Black was the last bar at the ski resort to close each night, and a frequent late-night hangout for instructors.

"What? No, I wish. We just talked a bunch, that's all." Helen was a little on the heavy side of athletic, but retained a bright cheery disposition that lightened the mood in any conversation. "I wish he'd pay some attention to me; I'd let him yank this zipper, that's for sure." With that, Helen zipped her bib up over her large bosom, and pulled the straps over her shoulders.

"I wish you the best with that. Maybe if he started dating you, he'd finally leave me alone. I'm sick and tired of him following me around like a lost puppy!" Both girls laughed at the mental image. Her left foot finally slid into the boot. She shifted her haunches and prepared to don the boot's mate. "Maybe we could set up some sort of double-date, you, me, Alex, and Demetri."

"Yeah, that would be perfect. I could really use a night of watching Demetri fawn all over you. No, I think I'll pass, but thanks for the offer."

Mia considered this while grunting. Her right ankle slipped into the boot, and she breathed a sigh of relief. "Okay, you're probably right. I wish I knew what I could do to help."

"If I think of anything, I'll let you know. In the meantime, I'm going to head up for the morning meeting; I still haven't signed in." Most instructors would sign in as they walked in the door, but if there was a line at the computer they might wait until after they had gotten dressed for the day. Helen rose up and began working her way down the aisle, a procedure considerably more difficult while wearing stiff ski boots.

Helen approached Demetri and Alex. "Oh, hi, Demetri," she said as she reached them. Demetri gave no reply, but turned and started working down the aisle, blocking Helen's progress.

"Hey, Helen," Alex responded. "How was your night?"

"Good, really good. Demetri and I got kinda drunk out at the Double Black. But there's no cure for a hangover like a faceshot, right?"

"Yeah, you got that right. But he's in a pretty foul mood today, despite the snow. I don't know what's gotten into his snowpants."

"Well, whatever it is, I hope he gets it worked out." Helen looked down at Alex, who was busy putting inserts into his helmet to block the airflow. "How about you? Everything going alright?"

"Yeah, great! Can you keep a secret?" Helen and Alex had gone to high school together, and remained friends ever since. They had talked each other into joining the ski school this winter, and encouraged each other throughout the initial training.

"Of course! My lips are sealed!"

Helen's mischievous grin gave Alex pause, but he forged ahead anyway. "Mia and I have been talking.... We're going to elope as soon as the season ends. We're talking about spending the summer in Idaho, but haven't decided where we'll go next winter."

"What? You're not coming back here?" Helen was dumbfounded, then her brain caught up with her. "I mean, congratulations!"

"Sssshhhh... It's a secret, nobody knows yet." Alex thought for a second. "And you're not going to tell them!"

Helen pointed a finger at her chest. "Moi?"

"Yes, you." Alex gave her finger a light smack. "Look, George doesn't know, and he'd shit a brick if he found out. He's mad enough that we're dating."

"How come it's never easy?"

Alex placed his helmet on his head and picked up his gloves. "Because if it were easy, they'd call it snowboarding." The pair laughed and started moving towards the front of the room. It was time for the morning meeting.

# 8:15 AM

# Suicide Rock

Any true snow fanatic will tell you the best run of the day is the first run. The line for the chairlift is longest in the early morning; true fans will wait an hour for the opportunity to ride "first chair" to the summit. The snow is untouched, the crowds have yet to congeal on the popular runs, and the energy is at its peak. A ski resort may run on Pabst Blue Ribbon in the afternoon, but it runs on coffee in the morning. Coffee, and occasionally a bit of whiskey. The whiskey is solely for flavor, of course.

For this reason the morning meeting is always a tense affair for ski and snowboard instructors. Everyone begins the meeting dressed in boots and gloves, and verbose speakers are shunned by the attendees. Any meeting that hasn't finished by the time the rope drops on the chair is a sin against snow. At Ridge Mountain Ski Resort, lessons began at 9AM sharp, which meant instructors would always have an hour of "warm-up" time before they had to teach children to walk like ducks and fend off the advances of middle-aged divorcees who convinced themselves to try something, or someone, new. Some of the more dedicated instructors would scout the mountain, picking terrain for lessons they planned to teach that day. Many of the older and wiser instructors would spend the time stretching their legs on slow controlled runs down intermediate slopes, letting their bodies adjust to the new day. Ron frequently spent it flinging himself off Suicide Rock.

Suicide Rock was a scraggly, ugly, twenty five foot boulder that sat above one of the more popular runs. Often the landing would be packed out and dangerous, but when a good storm came in it was like jumping onto a deep pile of freshly-plumped pillows. Suicide Rock could only be reached by means of a steep narrow hidden path through the trees, known only to staff and a handful of regulars, and even then most of them chose to pass it by for safer, saner joys on the mountain.

Ron stood at the top of the rock looking down. It was important to check one's landing to ensure one didn't land on another person, or more painfully, a rock exposed by the wind. Because Suicide Rock dropped into the edge of a run, more than once Ron had found a gaper resting in the depression caused by his frequent impacts. This time his diligence paid off, as he saw the bottom half of a ski sticking out of the snow directly where he was planning to land.

Ten feet downhill he saw Helen climbing up the groomed surface, one ski over her shoulder. What had happened was painfully clear; attracted by the new snow, Helen had left the corduroy to play in the powder on the side of the slope, only to have her tips dive in Ron's landing depression, which had been covered by the wind-driven snow. He was about to call down to her to check if she needed help when Demetri stopped above her with an abrupt hockey stop, spraying her with snow.

Demetri pulled off his goggles. "You alright?"

"Yeah, I just caught a snow snake." Helen laughed at her little joke. She mostly worked with kids, and the snow snake was a trick she used to keep the children from blaming themselves for tumbling, and losing confidence. Rather than telling children what they did wrong, it was sometimes more productive to let them use the fictitious excuse that they tripped over a white snow snake that they hadn't seen. Sometimes the children would go further, claiming that the snake had bitten them while they were skiing.

"You haven't seen Alex and Mia around have you?"

Helen stabbed her remaining ski into the snow, where it stuck up into the air like a flat telephone pole. She turned and began wading through the powder toward the wayward plank. "No, they're probably making out on the chairlift again."

Demetri grunted. "Jeez, Alex didn't turn in his class card from the homeschool group yesterday. I forgot to ask him about it in the locker room this morning. If you see him, could you let him know?"

Helen tugged uselessly at her ski, then switched to digging it out. "Sure, anything you want. What about Mia? Want me to pass a message to her, too?"

"No, that's alright. I just want to talk to her, try to get her to drop that deadweight loser Alex."

Helen was conflicted. She adored Demetri, but didn't like the idea of him meddling with her friend Mia's love life. On the other hand, Demetri was one of the senior instructors, and if he said Alex was a deadweight loser, he would know. Her train of thought was interrupted by the ski coming loose, and she began wading back towards Demetri. "Why not let her be? She'll discover her own mistakes soon enough."

"Not soon enough for me," retorted Demetri.

"What's that supposed to mean?"

"You know we were dating for a while, right?" Helen nodded. "I guess it's no secret that I still have feelings for her. I want her back."

Helen's heart dropped. She had known Demetri still had a crush on Mia, but it hurt to hear him say it. "Forget about her, you need to move on. Find another girl."

Demetri scoffed derisively. "Like who?"

There was a pause as Helen summoned up the courage to say what she'd be trying to say for weeks. This hardly seemed like the right place, but the time had come. "Me."

"You? You're joking, right?"

Tears began welling up inside Helen's eyes, and the emotional dam burst. "Yes, me! Come on, Demetri! I love you, give me a chance!"

"Love me? How can you say that? At best you've got a childish crush."

"I do love you! I do! Just give me a week, a night even, and I'll prove it to you!"

"Helen, my heart belongs to Mia. I could never love another, and certainly not you."

By this point Helen had lost all control of her faculties. She stood on the slope, one ski sticking straight up and the other askew at her feet, making a perfect spectacle of herself. "I'll do things for you that Mia could never dream of. Anything you want... Do you want to tie me down? Whip me? I'll do it anytime, anywhere for you. Please Demetri, I'm begging you!"

"You're making a fool of yourself, Helen. It makes me sick just to hear this. Stay away from me." Demetri made an abrupt skate to turn back down the hill, and quickly shot off away from the sobbing Helen.

Ron watched this from above. He debated trying to comfort Helen, but that would require admitting that he had overheard the entire conversation. He didn't know Helen very well, and imagined that the thought of a coworker listening in to her confessions would do little to make her feel better. Instead, he waited silently for a few moments as she put on her skis, and watched as she skied slowly off.

Then he hopped several feet up onto a small ramp, and flung himself off Suicide Rock.

# 8:45 PM

# Snow Sports School Main Office

Goblin was one of those snowboard instructors who got into the business for the free lift tickets. Technically he got into the business because he parents told him he needed to either get a job or get out of the house, and a winter job that allowed him to snowboard was more appealing than flipping burgers. He was now twenty-three, and how he had managed to keep this job for so long was a mystery to even him. He frequently arrived late, and found himself on the receiving end of a counseling nearly every week.

But Goblin, who never used his real name Rob, led the ski school for repeat business. He had built himself a clientele of students, mostly middle-aged women, who would schedule him personally for lessons. It might have been the short purple mohawk, the eyebrow ring, or the deep blue eyes. Perhaps it was his devil-may-care attitude. What was clear was these women were willing to part with their money to spend an hour or two in his company. The resort knew how much business he brought to the slopes, and was reluctant to rein him in.

Goblin led the school in another statistic as well – complaints. Not every woman appreciated his hands-on approach to instruction, and more than a few had complained about his hands on their hips, helping to demonstrate the proper position for snowboarding. Goblin didn't worry about them; they were overly sensitive. For the most part he was oblivious to the longer stares of divorcees and cougars, and he continued to just be Goblin.

Goblin didn't know why he was asked to come see George today. He suspected it was Sarah's father. He had taught a young lady how to snowboard the previous weekend. The lesson had gone well, and it was obvious that the young lady had natural talent for the sport. After two hours, she was riding comfortably down the beginner slopes, and he was confident that she would ask for a repeat lesson in the near future. As he handed Sarah her card at the end of the day, she reached up a suddenly kissed him on the lips. It was a chaste kiss that caught Goblin completely by surprise, and before he could react, her father materialized between them.

Her father ranted and raved like a sailor. Apparently the girl was only sixteen, and he had no ears for Goblin's protestations about who kissed who. Not only did Goblin not get any repeat business from the lesson, but he was stiffed out of a tip... unless you counted the kiss, of course. There was no way the resort could have missed the confrontation, so Goblin fully expected that this was his punishment for his latest indiscretion. It wasn't fair – this time he hadn't even done anything untoward.

He knocked on George's door and walked in.

"Shut the door behind you," George asked, finishing up a change to the charts on his desk. Goblin shut the door more often than he left it open. "Take a seat."

Goblin sat down, and crossed his legs. He twirled his upraised foot in a circle, impatiently waiting for his counseling.

"Look, Goblin, I've received a complaint, and I feel we need to discuss this." Goblin made no reaction. He'd long since learned that denial and arguing made the process longer and more painful. "I received a complaint from a guest that you were urinating outside."

Goblin's jaw dropped. He had been expecting to be yelled at about Sarah, not for having to take a piss. "Wha? I...?"

"We know it was you. There aren't many ski instructors with purple mohawks. In fact," George pretended to flip through some papers, "you're the only one we've got."

"When was this?" Goblin, like most skiers and snowboarders, would occasionally urinate outdoors. The restrooms were sparse on some parts of the mountain, but trees were plentiful.

"Last Sunday. We got the complaint late in the day, after you left."

Goblin thought. Yes, he had gone on Nine Ball around lunchtime. "Yes, but I was in the middle of a two-hour lesson! I couldn't just make the student sit and wait while I spend a half hour skiing to the lodge, do my business, then ski back to him?"

George shook his head. "Look, it's one thing to pee in the woods. But don't do it wearing the uniform. When you wear that uniform, you're an ambassador of this mountain to the public."

"Even ambassadors have to pee sometimes!"

"Go before your lesson. Surely you can make it two hours without having to use the restroom."

"Come on, man, what else am I gonna do? You gotta answer the call of nature!"

George dropped his pen onto the desk in exasperation. "You were in the middle of a lesson with a ten-year-old kid!"

"Trust me, ten-year-old kids know what peeing is. It wasn't anything new to him."

"You were in the middle of Ball Nine! For crying out loud, you weren't even in the woods!"

Goblin shrugged, clearly not understanding why

31

George was so worked up. "So what, the kid complained?"

"Not exactly..." George paused for effect. "One of the other guests did."

"There was nobody else around!"

"Actually, there was. You peed on a lift tower, Goblin. There were people on those chairlifts."

For some reason Goblin hadn't even considered looking up. He had been holding it in as long as he could, and about halfway down Nine Ball, when he realized there was nobody around. He never even thought about the fact that Nine Ball switched back and forth under Chair Nine, and that convenient post that was slightly off the run was in fact a lift tower, which meant forty people per minute were whisking by directly above him. He didn't know what to say.

"Listen, Goblin, I'm going to make this as plain as I can. If you're on the clock or wearing that uniform, you will find a way to get to a restroom. I don't care what you do wearing your own jacket on your free time, but not in uniform. Got it?"

Goblin nodded.

"Say it for me."

"I won't go to the bathroom outside in uniform."

"Thanks." George picked up his pen and

returned to his chart. "That's all I have. Have a good day out there."

Goblin opened his mouth to ask about Sarah, then thought better of it. Without a word he stood up and walked out of the office.

Under a chairlift, of all places!

# 9:30 AM
## Sunbeam Slope

There is certainly a lot of science that goes into being a ski instructor. A good ski instructor is an expert in physiology, understanding how each muscle and bone move to create different motions, positions, and pressures inside the boot. He is also an expert in physics, understanding how the sidecut of the ski causes turning forces when centripetal forces bend the center of the ski outward in a turn. He is also an expert in mountain weather forecasting, because he will be expected to know where the best slope conditions are at any given time.

But a great ski instructor is always an expert in psychology. Providing the best lesson to a student requires a detailed knowledge of the thoughts that are going through their mind. For most students, this means learning to help them work through fears and building trust, so that you can communicate and be understood. Many children seem to exhibit no fear, but can present communication challenges of their own. Many a child has come for a lesson without knowing exactly which part of his body was the calf, or even the ankle, so often pointing and demonstrating is required.

Adults are usually attentive and willing to listen. Kids usually want to learn, but given the choice they'd rather learn by experimentation than listening to someone talk. You need to find a way to catch and hold their interest, to captivate their attention, to make them want to listen to you. Mia was an expert in communicating with children, which led her to becoming one of the school's children's specialists. The majority of Mia's lessons were under ten years old, and she liked it that way. Children were more unpredictable, more fun, and the parents tended to tip very well.

Although Mia generally had a full dance card with by-name request private lessons, she did teach a regular weekly group of children. The Saturday morning program was the largest program on the mountain, and every instructor who could teach children was needed to make it work. Mia enjoyed working in a group environment as a change of pace, and she liked knowing that she would see the same children every week so that she could build a cohesive lesson plan over a season.

Mia's group had been working their way up from nothing, and she had decided they were ready for their first run down an intermediate slope. The "blue slopes", as they were known, were just steep enough that an out of control person could get seriously injured. Before the group could move up to this challenge, Mia had to ensure that everyone was capable of controlling their speed and not letting gravity take over completely. She had spent the morning reviewing and drilling on beginner slopes, and every indication was the group was skiing as well or better than the previous week.

The new soft snow helped, of course. Unlike old snow which could glaze over into a layer of ice under the effect of the sun's rays, the new snow would deform under the passage of each ski. This in turn would absorb some of the energy from the skier and slow him down. The dampness of the snow also made it somewhat sticky, further reducing speeds and increasing control. Today was the best conditions possible for a move onto new and exciting terrain.

Mia stood at the top of the Sunbeam Slope, addressing the six young children. She patiently explained that given the larger size of this slope, and the more difficult terrain, it was important that they all stay together. She explained that she would ski in the rear, and yell "Stop!" loudly if anyone were to fall. Everyone would then stop immediately, so the group wouldn't separate. She also explained that they were all to ski very slowly on this first run on unfamiliar terrain, and they could come back and do it again faster later if they wanted to.

She had the children repeat these rules back aloud, because you never really knew when they were listening.

And then she said go.

Gabe and Jose took off, twin lightning bolts headed down the slope. Mia sighed; there was no way the group could hope to keep up with those two. "STOP!" she yelled, to no avail. They were already out of earshot.

She looked at the other four who were moving along very slowly, using an exaggerated wedge to creep down the slope. They wouldn't fall, and even if they did, there was no way they would injure themselves at their snail pace.

"Alright, look, I have to go catch those two. We'll meet at the bottom of the run, on the left side of the slope by the last tree. I'll see you there, okay?"

There was a general murmur of agreement from the group, most of who were looking at their feet. Mia prayed they made it down alright, and began rapid skate down the hill. She had three advantages over the speed demons. First, her heavier mass meant she was sucked down by gravity much more. Second, her skis were designed for much higher speeds than the children's, including a recent waxing. Third, she knew how to skate, and could move much faster than one just riding the skis. Before long she was pushing forty miles an hour and rapidly catching up to the misbehaving students.

"STOP!" she yelled again, just as uselessly. The two were clearly engaged in a race at this point. Tucked down, poles snug against their sides, they followed one another in a straight line down the hill. Mia had to check her speed to avoid passing them up completely, but they were still moving far too fast to be safe. "STOP NOW!" They continued to ignore her. Mia cursed under her breath.

She knew she had to do something before the situation got any worse. She could grab one by the arm, and haul him to a stop. It was a difficult maneuver, especially with a resisting subject, and there was a risk of injury in a fall. Furthermore, that left one child hurtling down the mountain unsupervised. She could speed ahead to stop and try to block their path, but if they hit her they could both be very seriously injured. No immediate solutions came to mind.

Jose was trailing Gabe by about twenty feet when his right ski went squirrelly. Instead of tracking straight down the mountain as he intended, it began wobbling left and right rapidly, fishtailing in the snow. He couldn't regain control, and less than a second after it started he fell forward. The cause of the fishtailing became apparent; he had unbuckled his boot earlier to relax his foot and never retightened it. The boot was already too large for him, and unbuckled his foot sloshed around in it. When he fell, his entire foot slipped out of the boot, which remained affixed to the ski. He cartwheeled down the slope for twenty feet before coming to a rest at the side of the groomed surface.

Skis are designed to release the boot in a fall in order to minimize the risk of injury. Cleverly, they are also designed to extend brakes to stop the ski if the boot is removed, thus keeping the skis near their owner. Jose's boot, however, remained in the ski, and the ski continued to fly downhill. "Shit," said Mia. She lost sight of the ski as she stopped next to Jose's prone body.

"Are you okay?"

Jose opened his eyes and produced a giant grin. "That was AWESOME! Can we do it again!"

Mia sighed. "Get up, I'm going to have to get Gabe." She looked downhill, but could see neither Gabe nor the errant ski. "Do you know where your ski went?"

"Nut-uh."

Mia groaned. There was nothing in the training that covered this. It could take a half hour to find Jose's ski. Would Gabe wait that long at the bottom? Or would he wander off, or head back up the lift to ski some more, and end up who knows where? Losing children was not considered a good career move for a ski instructor. But could she leave Jose standing here for the fifteen minutes it would take to find Gabe and get back here? Mia looked down and saw Jose's foot, encased in a red and black sock. Dammit.

Salvation arrived a second later as a red-jacketed ski patroller stopped next to the pair. "Is everything alright?" he asked.

Mia didn't hesitate. "This is Jose. His other ski went downhill from here; the boot is still in so it's probably gone into the woods somewhere. I've got four more kids higher up the hill, and I need to grab one more that's headed to the bottom." She didn't wait for a response; she was afraid he would refuse to help. She quickly turned and skated down the hill without looking back.

She quickly reached the bottom of the mountain and scanned the crowd. Being the festival weekend, there were far more people than normal. Still, Gabe should stand out as a child alone, and she couldn't see him anywhere. After scanning the crowd, she looked over to the lifts. There were two lifts, each rising up to a different part of the mountain. If he took the wrong lift, it might take hours to find Gabe. Mia realized that keeping Gabe from taking a lift was more important than finding him immediately, and headed toward the first lift.

Mia skated through the dense crowd of the first lift, but couldn't find him. She knew time was running out. She pushed through the crowd and headed to the second lift. Scanning the line proved fruitless, until she saw Gabe standing at the front of the line. Still wearing her skis, she jumped out of line and skated as fast as she could to the front. A metal temporary fence, similar to the ones used to direct cattle, separated her from the crowd. Gabe was moving forward to get on the chair swinging around to pick him up. Without thinking, she dove over the railing and grabbed the back of Gabe's jacket, pulling him to the ground.

Nick heard the commotion and turned his head. This was his third year of liftie duty, making him a veteran by any measure, but he had never seen anyone leap over the railing and grab a customer like that. He immediately pressed the emergency stop button, and ran over. "Let go of that kid!"

Mia had lost all sense, and was focused entirely on getting broken class back together in one place. "He's MINE!" she growled, hauling him skis and all back over the railing.

Nick recognized Mia as one of the instructors, and paused. "Um, you really shouldn't do that. Someone could get hurt...."

"If this kid goes up that lift, I promise someone will get hurt." She looked down at Gabe. "And YOU are in big trouble mister!"

Gabe was at crossed emotions. On one hand, that run was easily the single best, most exciting experience of his entire life. On the other hand, the nice woman who taught the class suddenly looked willing and able to tear him apart and scatter the pieces across the mountain. He decided to hide his grin and go along with her to the tree on the far side of the run.

Mia and Gabe had just gotten to the tree where they had agreed to meet when she saw a ski patrolling descending the hill with five children trailing behind him. Mia counted them twice, but they were all there, including Jose on two skis. The group came to a stop next to her.

"Oh my God thank you so much!" she exclaimed. "How on Earth did you find the ski?"

The patroller shrugged. His jacket proclaimed him to be Jim; in her haste Mia hadn't noticed that before. "It was sitting at the edge of the run about fifty feet down. His sock got a little wet though."

"I can't thank you enough. Can I get you a round at the bar tonight or something?"

"Nah, just doing my job."

"Maybe, but I certainly owe you something for that."

The patroller looked at Mia's uniform. "Mia?" Mia nodded. "It's obvious that you're having a very bad day. I'm just glad I could help out a little." With that, he waved to the kids, and skated back toward the lift.

Jose looked up at Mia. "Can we do that again,

Mia? Can we?"

# 10:00 AM
## Resort President's Office

The mountain range shares a lot of blood with the ocean. Many fear to cross it, and most do so only by plane. And while most consider it a barrier and a nuisance, there are those who are called to it by a voice they cannot silence. To them, the mountains have a siren song that compels them to spend more time upon them until they cannot comprehend life on flat ground.

Like the ocean, the mountains feel the tides pulling at them. During the day, anabatic winds push up the mountainside. The exposed peaks are warmed by the sun, causing the air to rise above the mountain. The low pressure above the summit sucks warm air up from the valley floor, causing a gentle upslope breeze that can last all day. Conversely, at nighttime, katabatic winds produce the opposite effect as cold air rushes down the slopes at night, dropping temperatures and wind chill factors to dangerous levels.

The customers of Ridge Mountain Ski Resort formed another tide, a tide of snowsuits, helmets, and lattes. They came in the morning in a great mass, taking the resort from deserted to packed in a matter of hours. They would move about, up and down, all day long, before being transported in bulk at nightfall from the slopes to the bars. The après-ski bars, lounges, and hot tubs would contain them until shortly after midnight, when they mysteriously vanished, only to reappear the following morning.

The brotherhood of the ocean and the mountain were not lost on Theo. He was born in Aspra Spitia, Greece, and raised on the Mediterranean. Once he was old enough, he began work for his father, operating a large fishery. While his father preferred him to work indoors grooming him to eventually take over the company, Theo would find an excuse at least once a week to spend the day at sea fishing with the men.

In 1976, the Parnassos Ski Center opened, not far from his town. Theo was twenty two at the time, and fascinated by this new sport. Austria hosted the Winter Olympics that year, and Theo watched enthralled as skiers raced down the mountain at high speed on his small black and white television. He was immediately hooked his first time out, and began spending his weekends on snow. In 1988 his father passed on, and he immediately sold the company to move to America – and live his dream of operating a major ski resort.

Ridge Mountain Ski Resort was a much smaller

operation when he purchased it, but with time and careful expansion, it had become a major regional destination. Although his fortunes wavered depending on the weather and the economy, he had done well for himself, as well as the thousands of people now employed by the resort during the winter.

None of this was on Theo's mind at the moment. Rather, he looked out his window, drank a sip of coffee, and allowed himself his first moment of relaxation of the day. The festival was on, and stress levels were much higher than normal. He had spent the entire morning dealing with countless issues of seemingly minor import, but nevertheless requiring his intervention or judgment. In theory his wife Lita had the reins for the festival, but the lines between festival operations, daily operations, and "strategic issues" were blurry, and when in doubt people ask the boss.

Lita knocked as she entered, more as a courtesy than anything else. She was his wife, but technically she was also an employee, and everyone saw that she got no special treatment professionally for her relationship with Theo.

"Theo, I need your input on the mountaintop burger blast tomorrow. The Forest Service denied our request to use the BBQs at the top of Chair Seven. I've filed a complaint about the short notice, but that won't help us now. I'm thinking the best thing to do would be to move the burger blast to the patio of the warming hut at the top of Chair Nine. There's no green run down from there, so we lose some traffic, but we can use the existing permit and at least we don't have to cancel it entirely."

Theo thought carefully while remaining focused out the window. "What about the restaurant on the South Peak?"

"We could do that," Lita conceded, "but the restaurant already sells burgers every day. It loses the 'cool' factor of a mountaintop BBQ. The guests like to think we're doing something special for them."

Theo nodded. He already knew he would agree to Lita's proposal, but he liked to hear the logic behind the request. "Go ahead, the warming hut will be fine. We'll have to work out something for trash removal, but that shouldn't be too hard."

Lita came up behind Theo and put her hand on his shoulder. "Theo... About George..."

Theo turned to look at his wife. "It's none of our business. That's it."

"Theo, George is practically family, and that makes it our business. He's making a mistake, and you have the responsibility of warning him."

"A father has the responsibility of finding a good husband for his daughters."

Lita took Theo's hand in her own. "No, they don't. Not anymore. Mia can love whoever she chooses."

Theo looked into Lita's eyes. "Was it so bad when our parents put us together? Did we not find love together?"

Lita squeezed his hand. "Of course we did, Theo. But that was in the old country. The ways were different there."

"George is from the old country, too, Lita."

"But Mia isn't. Mia was born here, and raised here. She has never even seen Greece except in old photographs. You can't ask her to abide by traditions of another culture."

Theo began to respond, but paused. Lita had a way of making her point when nobody else could get Theo to see. "But I can't ask George to turn his back on his own daughter. He must see that she is taken care of...."

"No, Theo, not here. In America, a father must see that his daughter can take care of herself."

Theo released Lita's hand and turned back to the window. He could see a class of young children being led to the learning area, and he watched to see if the instructor was maintaining control of the class. "Dammit, Lita." He took another sip of his coffee. From his vantage, the instructor appeared to be doing a good job, despite the large crowds. He wondered briefly who it was. "Alright, I'll talk to him. But no promises."

"Thank you, Theo." Lita rose onto her toes to kiss Theo gently on the cheek, then walked out of the office.

"Dammit."

# 11:00 AM

## Top of Chair Nine

The job of a lift attendant is a thankless one. Rarely does anyone ever stop to pat a liftie on the back, congratulate him on a job well done, or nominate him for employee of the week. Never in the history of Ridge Mountain Ski Resort had a guest given a cash tip to a lift attendant for ensuring that his ride to the top was a safe one, and the lift shack was no route to great fortune. Rather, Frank had suffered many of the slings and arrows of outrageous customers insulting him, berating him, and threatening to have his head impaled on a stake for running the lift too slow, too fast, or sometimes too high off the ground.

Loading the beginner lift was a tiring job that required constant attention. The lift had to be stopped frequently for "never-evers" trying to load for the first time, and at least once an hour a kid with bindings set wrong would lose a ski as they started to lift up into the air. The liftie would have to pick children up out of the snow and corral parents into their proper places on the chair, constantly vigilant for gapers bound and determined to hurt themselves on his watch.

Working the top of the advanced lift, on the other hand, gave Frank an opportunity to check Facebook and perform some quality navel-gazing. At the top of the chair, Frank had two primary duties. Every now and then he would go outside with a shovel and repair the glide zone the skiers and riders used to exit the lift. This consisted of throwing some snow onto the ramp and patting it down with the back of the shovel. His other duty was to maintain a close eye on patrons and immediately stop the lift if anyone fell trying to get off. This being the advanced lift, that didn't happen often, and he instead browsed the latest gossip on his cell. And drank coffee, of course.

Nick opened the door of the small lift shack and squeezed in. Frank hadn't seen him coming, but it had neither been posted on Facebook nor foretold in his coffee cup, so that wasn't surprising. It was time for shift change; Frank was about to start his lunch break, and then he would be moving to the top of Chair Seven to give someone else a chance to eat.

"Well met, my Lady," Frank said by way of greeting, "I trust that you are in good spirits?"

Nick sat on the spare stool and conjured up his best girl voice. "But a lady such as myself would never indulge in spirits, for they are an abomination and the devil's work!"

Frank laughed. "Your Shakespeare is really good. You'll knock them dead, you really will."

"I just wish I didn't have to be the girl. I've got a damn mustache! Girls don't have mustaches."

"The ones you date do." Nick smiled but made no comment, so Frank moved on. "So what, you want us to change it to a Bromance play? Romeo and Jonathon?"

Nick chuckled. "It'd certainly bring new meaning to swordplay."

"Oh, you're right. Perhaps we should redo it as a lesbian romance."

"Back to the mustache." Nick pointed at his brush. "Gotta do something about the mustache."

"No problem, we'll just have you perform in a handstand the whole time. Nobody will know the difference."

Nick's chuckle upgraded to full laughter. "I'd have the biggest nose you've ever seen on a lesbian."

"That you would, Nick. Just don't let it stick too far up."

"That could be a challenge if you surround me with beautiful lesbians."

Now it was Frank's turn to laugh. "Seriously, though, isn't *Romeo and Juliet* a little too sad? I mean, they both die at the end. Shouldn't we consider having them survive and make it a happy story?"

Nick had a confused look on his face. "Aren't we just going to do the balcony scene? Nobody dies in the balcony scene."

"Oh, right, I forgot."

"Haven't been studying your lines yet?"

"No, not yet." Frank shook his head. "Want to go over them while I eat? I've got some time, might as well spend it here."

"Sure, why not." Nick rummaged in his bag for the now somewhat soggy script.

"Hey, that gives me an idea... What if we did the entire play on the balcony?"

"Huh? What do you mean by that?"

"What if we condensed the entire plot into one scene, with one set? The entire *Romeo and Juliet* performed in five minutes on the balcony!"

"Well, that would certainly make the suicides more interesting... but I think Peter would go around the bend."

Frank pulled his lines out of backpack. "It would probably mean more lines for my faithful hound, though."

Nick laughed. "Ready to begin?" He returned to his girly voice. "Romeo, Romeo, wherefore art thou Romeo?"

"I hate that line! Can't I just yell 'Right here,

bitch!' up at her?"

"No, Frank, wherefore means why, not where."

"That doesn't make any sense at all."

"It's not supposed to make sense. It's Shakespeare. Okay, let's try it again from the top, and be serious this time!"

# 11:45 AM
# The Beyond

Skiing is lot like pizza. Some people prefer deep dish, some people prefer thin crust. Some people want plain cheese, some people want pepperoni, and some people want the works. There are even a few that want anchovies. But no matter how you prefer it, all pizza is good pizza.

It's also a lot like sex that way.

There are those who can bring a very snobbish attitude toward skiing, refusing to go out in anything but the best of conditions, powder hounds who insist that if you aren't at least waist deep in the soft stuff, you might as well be inside chugging a Pabst Blue Ribbon by the fire. These people have lost sight of the true joy of skiing.

At its heart, skiing is an expression of freedom. The skier can move fast or slow in whatever direction he chooses, even back uphill for limited distances. Sure, the hiker can do the same, but the skier doesn't rely on his own energy. Gravity pulls us down, but the skier harnesses it, controls it, and uses it to achieve his goals.

There's power in a ski carving underneath you. The tension in a loaded ski is strong enough that the leg can easily sense it; the skier feels the power of the carve. When done right, it's the feeling of taking a well-tuned sports car through a tight race track. With enough practice, a skier can wield immense power and control in even the iciest of conditions.

If hardpack is akin to a race car, deep powder is an airplane. Your skis don't slide across the surface of powder, but float inside the powder. There's no sensation of friction underfoot, but a feeling of flying. The ski generates lift that counteracts gravity, which combined with the buoyancy provided by the denser medium of snow, helps keep the skier from dropping too deep and getting stuck. With skill, the skier can use his speed and various movements to control his depth, moving smoothly up and down depending on the goals he wants to achieve. Rise up to make turning easier, drop down to scrub off some speed... Gone is the race car metaphor, and rising to take its place is the nimble fighter jet, moving in three dimensions.

All skiing may be good pizza, but good powder skiing is a deep dish Hawaiian pizza with chunks of smoked Pacific salmon. This is the ultimate.

Helen was enjoying the powder today. She

was forty-five minutes into a two hour private lesson where the guest had requested Helen teach him how to ski in powder. His name was Mike, and he had never been able to handle powder in the past. When they started, he was stiff in the powder, and as a result would quickly sink down and get tripped up, falling in the snow. Fortunately the landings were soft.

After a half hour Helen had been able to teach Mike the basics and overcome his fears, enabling him to glide through the shallower powder on the sides of the runs. Confident that Mike was capable of handling more difficult terrain, and wanting more time in the deeper snow herself, they had headed to The Beyond, where they now stood looking down on the already chopped but still deep powder. The lesson was good enough that Helen had all but forgotten about her breakdown earlier in the morning.

"Are you sure I can handle this?" Mike looked nervously at his feet, or at least where he would have seen his feet if they weren't buried.

"Absolutely. Remember, stay loose, let yourself bounce up and down, and make sure both feet work together for the turns. It's all about rhythm." A little repetition of the lesson was a good thing; much could be forgotten during a chairlift ride up a mountain. "I'll go ahead and make a few turns then stop. Focus on my legs, see how they move together in time with my turns." Mike nodded apprehensively. "Ready?" Mike nodded again, and Helen began a series of slow controlled turns, then stopped.

Helen looked up. There was some chop that could throw Mike off, but the snow was good, and Mike had improved dramatically, so she waved that he should come down. Mike started slow, but quickly gained speed in the steeper terrain. As his skis floated up, it was clear that he had remembered the lesson, and Mike soon stopped next to Helen with a giant grin on his face.

"Holy shit, that was fun! Let's go again!"

Helen laughed. "Sure, but we need to finish this run first. We're only a few turns in."

Mike suddenly looked concerned. "Hey, Helen, can I ask a favor?"

Helen's face suddenly became serious. "Sure, Mike, what can I do for you?"

"Look, I don't want to offend you. I've learned more in this lesson than in any other lesson I've ever had, and it's been way more fun. But now that I can ski powder, I don't really want any more lessons today. I'd like to just, well, enjoy this for a while."

Helen thought hard. She'd never had a student end a lesson early, and had no idea what the company's policy was. Would he be refunded the difference in price? Would she still get paid for the time? She had no idea.

Mike interrupted her thoughts. "I've got you

until one, so we still have an hour. Instead of doing a bunch of drills, could you spend that time showing me all the best powder runs? You know, the secret stashes that everyone else doesn't know about?"

Helen's smile returned. "Oh, yes, I can do THAT."

Mike grinned like a Cheshire cat. "Awesome! What are we waiting for?" Without waiting for his instructor, he took off down the snow.

Helen started after her charge. In her mind she thought this might be the best lesson ever, but that thought was quickly replaced by a much stronger, louder thought as she gained speed: Woot!

# 12:30 PM

# Top of Knife Edge Run

When lunch break comes around, most ski instructors will retire to the locker room, loosen their boots, crack open a thermos of hot cocoa and eat a baloney sandwich they had prepared the night before. The less fortunate instructors might have to make do with peanut butter and jelly; Warren Miller famously survived for years on saltine crackers and ketchup stolen from the condiments islands at ski resorts.

Snowboard instructors, on the other hand, are excited by the prospect of an hour of free riding. They shed their uniform jackets and rush to the lifts, eager to relieve the stress of the morning by making a few runs through the park, or in this case, through the deep pow that has clung to the edges of the slopes in the trees well into the day. Knife Edge Run was a steep double-black diamond with a harsh double fall line, situated so that if you drifted too far to the right you dropped down quickly and couldn't return to the right side. As the run continued, the open area on the left narrowed between the drop and the trees, until eventually you had no choice but to either dive between the pines or drop to the right. Few people continued beyond the narrow portion, which was exactly why Ron was planning to ride there now.

The cat track from the top of the lift to Knife Edge Run was flat with a slight rise in the middle, so he had skated there with one foot in the board. Sitting at the top, he reached down to strap himself in. It had been a stressful morning; he had taught one two-hour group lesson that seemed to consist entirely of Asian women with no sense of balance and poor English skills. Although Ron liked to consider making a chairlift run the goal of a first-day lesson, he considered himself lucky simply to have not required an ambulance to take any of these women down the hill.

He patted his pockets, and found what he was looking for. The valley was beautiful from this vantage point, and he debated lighting a joint to calm his nerves after the morning disaster. Getting caught doing drugs during the workday meant immediate termination, but many of the instructors had risked it on a stressful day. Still, today was a busy stressful day, and busy days meant you were more likely to get caught. Ron left the waterproof zipper sealing his pocket closed, and stood up to plan his route into the trees as his girlfriend Anna plopped down beside him.

"Going to look for powder in the trees?" Anna began buckling her boot into the binding. "I'm betting this board will rock in the deep stuff!" Anna had won the board she was riding the week before at a raffle to raise money for the Ski Patrol Canine Search and Rescue. The board was clearly too large for her slim frame, but she had won it, and that made it hers. Ron, on the other hand, was the perfect size for the board, and had told her this on more than one occasion.

"Come on, Anna, you know that board would fit me perfectly. I've got some old narrow rides I could trade you."

Anna stood up, having secured both feet. "Drop it, Ron. I won this fair and square, and it's mine. Why would I want to trade it for an old board? And a narrow one, at that? I need a powder board. Besides, it's pretty. It's got a dragon on it."

"Anna! It's just not right that you'd take a board that's too big for you when you know I need a new one!"

"Well, maybe if you didn't waste all your money on pot you could afford it. Come on, let's ride!" Anna started along the spine, heading directly for the trees.

Ron fumed. Although they had been dating since mid-summer, this snowboard had been a major point of contention for the last seven days. It seemed dumb to break up with a girlfriend over a snowboard, but on the other hand, what was the point of having a girlfriend that didn't care about your happiness? Either way, he wasn't going to allow her to get any virgin powder that might still be lurking in the trees, so he shot off after her, determined to beat her to the goods.

Anna had a head start and was moving quickly, and even given her lighter weight she was able to beat Ron to the trees. Unfortunately, she was going too fast on a board too heavy and wide for the narrow trees, and couldn't make the tight turns required to thread the needle's eye of pine trunks. She had barely gone five feet into the woods when the realization that she didn't have control hit her, and she overreacted, swinging the board quickly around and bringing it to a sudden stop. Momentum carried her forward and down the hill, passing the now stationary board and her feet, and she slammed face-first into the soft snow.

The light snow provided little resistance on the steep slope, and Anna slid down the slope. Almost immediately, she felt herself drop suddenly then stop, suspended upside down with her feet above her. Immediately she grasped the seriousness of the situation – she was trapped in a tree well, an empty cavity that forms under the canopy of a large tree during big storms. Her snowboard bridged the top of the well, bringing down a wave of snow with every movement she made. She took a deep breath a screamed at the top of her lungs for Ron.

Ron was close behind her and had seen the fall. "I'm here, hold still, I gotcha!" He finished removing his board and waded through waist deep fluff to the well. "Don't move, you'll only bury yourself. I'll dig you out." Not having his shovel with him, he used the snowboard to dig a path down into the side of the well. Trying to lift Anna straight out would just have collapsed the cavity, suffocating her in the snow.

"Jesus Christ, get me out of here!" Anna was not prone to panicking, but if there ever was a time to do it, this seemed like the time. Her better judgment kept enough hold to keep her still, trusting Ron to rescue her.

The snow was light and easy to move, so it took only a few minutes for Ron's digging to have the desired effect, and an angled ditch was created leading directly to Anna's head. Ron tossed his board aside and grabbed Anna, lifting her up and setting her down in the ditch. She immediately sat up, and nearly passed out from the sudden change of blood pressure in her head. She grabbed her helmeted head with her gloves. "Wow."

"I'll say. You could have been killed there."

"No shit. Thanks for saving me."

"Anytime, babe. You okay?"

Anna shook her head. "Yeah, I think so. Just a bit shaken up." She laughed at the little joke. "Gimme a second, and I'll be fine."

It was eerily quiet. The resort may have been crowded, but this run was near its edge, and snow has an amazing ability to absorb sound. "I, uh, don't think we should report this to ski patrol."

Anna nodded. "God, I hate paperwork."

"Plus they'd probably close the run, and it's one of my favorites."

"Yeah, that too."

Ron reached for his board and began strapping it on. "Anyway, I told you that board is too big for you. You can't control it."

Anna snapped her head up. "What? I nearly died and you're going to use it to try to take my board from me? Fuck you, Ron!"

Ron looked up at Anna, clearly confused. "No, Anna, that's not it. I'm just trying to look out for you because I care!"

"Whatever, asshole. I can look after myself." Anna stood up and crawled out of the ditch. "I'll see you around; you don't need to follow me down." She hopped her board to face down the slope and began riding through the trees, slower than before but still perhaps too fast.

Ron sat in the snow. He wasn't sure what pissed off Anna so much. He really did worry for her safety...

that snowboard was too large for her, and she was bound to get hurt if she insisted on riding it. The fact that it was perfect for him wasn't the only reason he wanted her to give it up.

# 12:55 PM
## Lesson Meeting Area

There are different theories when it comes to organizing a children's school. One common and intuitive structure is to hire separate instructors for the adult school and the children's school. This provides children's instructors who are dedicated to working with children. However, it stymies their professional development as the Professional Ski Instructors Association, which certifies instructors for meeting minimum standards, tests applicants across a wide range of potential guests. One can apply for and receive a "Children's Specialist" certification, but you must still study for and test with adult students to receive the more valuable "level" certifications. Additionally, such a system produces inefficiencies as one school or the other may become overworked while other instructors are idle, due to the natural variability of the workload. This system is popular at the largest resorts, where the schools can be so large that physically moving between them can be exhausting.

A competing strategy is to have a single pool of

instructors, and assign them daily to various work centers. This centralizes manpower and training, and provides instructors an opportunity to develop their skills with all types of students. But it can be frustrating for an instructor who specializes in working with senior citizens to be paired with a group of six-year-olds. Very young children's lessons often run on a different schedule, further complicating things. Smaller resorts often use this model to minimize the number of instructors they need to hire.

Many mid-sized resorts find compromise solutions, where some instructors are permanently assigned to the children's school while others may flex there as needed. Ridge Mountain Ski Resort was such a resort. The concept worked really well, until weekends like the festival where both schools were overwhelmed by lessons.

When things really got moving, private lessons and children's lessons would get priority. The private lessons simply because they paid so much more, and the children's lessons because you couldn't go beyond a certain student-instructor ratio without losing control of a class, or worse, losing a student altogether. Adults in group lessons would generally understand when they were placed in a large group on a holiday weekend, but not when their six-year-old was in the same predicament.

The undermanned group lesson desk meant most group lesson instructors were taking a lesson at every lineup, and most lessons were large. The one o'clock lineup was traditionally the busiest, and most of the instructors arrived early to help deal with the throng of guests who would appear.

Alex did not have the experience or knowledge required to be assigned to the private lesson desk, and felt fortunate today to not be assigned to the children's school. Despite the large crowd already forming, he felt lucky to be here rather than surrounded by a hundred screaming children. Adults he could handle.... Children were another story entirely.

Alex saw a group of children returning to the school with their facilitators. The facilitators were mostly teenaged girls. They weren't instructors, but would supervise the children getting to and from the class, help them get dressed, and prepare their meals. Depending on the size of the class, one or two would stay with the younger groups to help with potty breaks, meltdowns, and other inevitable issues.

The group moved as a train, each child holding the child in front of him. The lead facilitator, a young girl Alex didn't recognize, was making choo-choo noises as they moved past the adult lesson meeting area. He watched as the child at the back of the train, playing the caboose, let go of the train and bent down to pick up some snow. He made a rough imitation of a snowball, and let fly directly at Alex.

Alex ducked, causing the missile to fly over his head. He heard the impact behind him, and turned around to see Goblin, face covered in snow.

"Hoser!" exclaimed Goblin, who reached down and armed himself. Alex moved out of the line of fire just quickly enough to see Goblin throw the snowball inches above the kid.

"You!" came a voice out of nowhere. "You with the snowball!"

Alex and Goblin both turned around to see Phil running across the snow at top speed. Phil was the Public Relations Director for Ridge Mountain Ski Resort. Whenever it snowed, his job was working with television news stations to convince them that "There's snow in the mountains!" would make a great news story, and yes, they could use the ski resort as a location to film. He was returning from an interview with Channel Four when he saw Goblin throw a snowball at a young child.

Panting, he reached Goblin and poked him in the chest, a brave move against a man with a mohawk and a facial piercing. Phil was the youngest member of the management team at thirty-two, and as part of his job he exuded an image of 'hip'. He wore his dark hair short but sported a well-trimmed goatee, and was never seen without ski pants and a Ridge Mountain logo jacket, even in the office. He was rarely seen upset, since his image of Ridge

Mountain Ski Resort was that of a happy place. "You just threw a snowball at a kid! I'm going to have to speak to your supervisor; there's no snowball throwing permitted at Ridge Mountain!"

Goblin held a finger to his reddened cheek. "He hit me first."

"I don't care! No employee, especially not one wearing a uniform jacket, is going to throw snowballs at this resort. What if someone got injured? Can you imagine the lawsuit? It's totally-" Phil was cut off by a snowball slamming into the side of his face. Alex, watching amusedly from the side, laughed out loud.

"What the-?" Phil was beside himself. He saw the attacker, no more than six years old, pressing his thumb to his nose and wiggling his fingers. Phil grabbed a clump of snow and instinctively hurled it at the brat.

Tab, a young facilitator working to pad out her application for college, spotted the young caboose who had derailed from the train. She bent down to pick him up when Phil's snowball hit her square in the arse. The instigator laughed at first, but was quickly dropped to the ground as Tab turned to return fire.

Tab didn't recognize Phil, and she had been texting with her friends during the Rules & Regulations brief at the hiring seminar. She didn't know who the man was that had hit her, but her aim was good and she nailed him in the chest.

The rest of the train had turned at the caboose's

laughter and saw Tab throw a snowball into the instructor corral. A cacophony of laughter and screaming erupted as the children began indiscriminately firing snowballs at the instructors.

The general public began clearing the area, remaining close enough to watch but far enough away to avoid stray shots. On one side the facilitators became a human shield, with children hiding behind them and throwing snowballs at the instructors. The other side consisted of a large lineup of instructors, unleashing white fury at the facilitators, who feebly attempted to return fire themselves.

It was an unfair fight from the very beginning. As the instructors began gaining ground, advancing toward the children, Tab realized they had no chance. She called a hasty retreat, and the children fled into the children's school while the facilitators laid down covering fire. She remained out with three other facilitators, now hopelessly outgunned. "Inside!" she yelled, tapping her friends on the shoulders to alert them to the retreat.

Goblin and Alex led the chase, snowballs whistling over their heads as they ran. They fired final parting shots as the girls entered the building, then turned to walk back to the meeting area, faces beaming.

"I don't care what that upper-management

douche says, that was awesome!" said Goblin, wrapping his arm over Alex's shoulders as they walked. "We ought to have daily snowball fights here."

Alex playfully tossed his last snowball into Goblin's stomach. "Don't count on it, Goblin. We'll probably catch hell for that. Speaking of which, where did Phil go?"

"Who?"

"Phil. The Director of Public Relations? The guy who was chewing you out until he threw the snowball at that kid?"

Just then Alex was hit in the back by a snowball thrown hard from behind him. He wheeled around to see Tab smiling out the window of the children's school. Another window opened, and another snowball sailed into the group of instructors. The fight was back on!

This time the fight was much more fair. Although still heavily outnumbered, the windows provided excellent protection from incoming fire. Ammunition was limited by the rate at which they could ferry snow in through the back door, although soon they were able to supplement their stocks with snow fired in by the instructors.

For several minutes the instructors traded continuous fire with the children and facilitators. There were a few casualties for the benefit of the children, where an instructor would be hit and theatrically fail about before falling to the snow, his last words cut off by a finishing shot. The snowboard instructors had erected a wall of snowboards to provide a safe haven, and moved some of the injured into its relative safety. The air was filled with the whomping of snow on jackets, the laughter of children, and the occasional cry of "Medic!"

"What in the name of... Stop! Everyone stop right now!" George looked over the scene. Instructors throwing snowballs at guests? He looked at his watch. The lineup should have already begun, but everyone had fled the meeting area. He was beside himself with rage.

Phil was beside George as well, having fetched him to stop the fight from snowballing out of control. "See? I told you!" he cried.

"Shut up," George growled. He was busy memorizing the faces of everyone involved so he could yell at each of them personally later today. Right now he had a lineup to bring back onto schedule. "Into the corral, all of you! This is totally inappropriate! You know the rules concerning snowballs!"

There was a quiet voice, but a voice that cut through George's harsher tones. "George."

George turned. It was Lita, walking up behind him. "Be with you in a minute, Lita."

"No, George." She walked right up to him,

and lowered her voice so that the instructors couldn't hear. "You run the ski school, but I run the Snow Festival. And what I just saw was exactly the kind of spirit we're looking for at the Snow Festival."

George couldn't believe his ears. The snowball rule wasn't his rule; it was a company-wide policy for legal reasons. "But Lita, the liability!"

"Damn the liability, George. Let people have a little fun once in a while. Look at the guests. Look at them." George did. "You too, Phil. Look at their faces." Phil, who had been pretending not to eavesdrop, turned to look at the guests. "Don't they look happy? Happy instructors mean happy guests, and happy guests mean a successful festival."

George didn't like this at all. Rules were laid down by the leaders, and he followed them. It wasn't his place to go against what the boss had put down. But Theo had put Lita in charge of the Snow Festival. In any case, there didn't seem to be any point in arguing this now.

"Alright, Lita. But just this once. If I see this again, I'll be suspending instructors."

"Thank you, George." Lita turned in her snow boots and started walking toward the management offices. "See you around!"

# 2:10 PM

# Snow Sports School Locker Room

Snow sports instructors can be easily divided into two categories. There are those who take up the lifestyle for a chance to get free lift tickets and half-price chow at the cafeteria, and there are those who know there is no better feeling than sharing the love of snow, knowing that someone has learned how to experience ecstasy that comes from having complete freedom and power on snow. Skiing or riding, when done well, is best described as "flying". It's certainly the closest you can get while still being in contact with the ground, and the sensations are surprisingly similar.

When it's raining, it's clear to see who falls into which category. Some instructors hide in the back, hoping they will be able to spend the day dry in the locker room. Others will push to the front, hoping for an opportunity to take a rewarding lesson that will make a miserable day worthwhile. On a powder day, the distinction becomes harder to see. Only the most selfless instructors would be happier helping a young child on the bunny hill when the deep powder beckons. Mia was one of those instructors.

Like many instructors on busy days, she had given up her lunch break to take on an additional lesson. A few granola bars can go a long way towards keeping an instructor on the snow for eight straight hours, and a water reservoir with a drinking tube can keep you hydrated. Mia's schedule had no breaks, and she liked it that way. But her current student was ten minutes late, and still counting.

Her previous class had been two young sisters, ages four and five, and a pair of absolute terrors. Three other ski instructors had tried to tame the girls without success, but there was something about Mia's personality, or maybe her smile, that made children immediately like her. During Mia's first lesson with the girls she had managed to get them up the chairlift for the first time, and they have followed her faithfully since. No-one else would even consider taking the class, but Mia enjoyed their company and continued to work them up to higher and higher levels. Today they had progressed to intermediate slopes for the first time, and the pride on their faces when they told their parents was worth more than any tip. Certainly better than the morning, when two of her boys decided to race to the bottom.

Mia glanced at her watch. Fifteen minutes was

the rule, and it was getting close. After fifteen minutes the instructor would report to management and the class would be officially canceled. The school offered partial refunds if the student called, even the same day. Simply not showing up cost the student the full class fee, yet it happened on a regular basis. The instructors who just wanted some money enjoyed getting paid for a class they didn't teach; Mia was frustrated that she lost an opportunity to teach a class.

She glanced at her watch again. It was two-fifteen; her student had officially skipped class. This student was an eight-year-old boy who spoke mostly French. He had missed several lessons because his parents would up and leave the country and take him with them, only to return the next week and apologize. They clearly could afford the lessons, but Mia felt common courtesy would require a simple phone call so that she wouldn't stand out in the cold for a quarter hour. She picked up her poles and skis and walked over to the school, leaning them against the rail provided for that purpose.

Inside the school, Mia walked directly to George Markos's office. "Hey Dad, my two didn't show."

George glanced at the spreadsheet covering his desk. "Pierre? That's the third time he's been a no-show."

"Yep, I think that's about right." Mia walked over to the mini-fridge in the corner of the office. "I've got a three, so if you don't mind, I'll just grab a sandwich and have a late lunch."

"Sure, go ahead."

Mia slathered a liberal coating of peanut butter onto a piece of bread, then sliced a banana on top of that. She folded the result into an odd calzone, and proceeded to eat the remainder of the banana.

"Take a seat, Mia, I'd like to chat with you for a bit."

Mia grabbed an off-brand sports drink, something that had been donated to the school as a promotional item. Various companies would frequently donate energy bars, drinks, and other goodies to ski schools, hoping the instructors would eat them in front of students, or even better, tell their students that those products were the best on the market. Sometimes it worked as intended, other times the products were so bad the instructors would give them away to students just to avoid eating them. She sat down opposite her father and continued to eat her lunch.

"Look, I want to talk to you about Demetri."

Mia put down the sports drink bottle. It had a picture of a hamster leaping over hurdles, with a giant grin on its face. "Come on, Dad, I told you that we're done with this discussion. The answer is no."

George folded his hands thoughtfully in front of him, as if he were trying to intimidate a junior instructor. It didn't work on his daughter. "I understand, Mia, but you need to understand as well. Demetri is a good man with a bright future. Alex is naïve and lacks ambition. Besides... Demetri is looking to marry you."

Mia gasped. "Marry me? We *broke up*! The guy is batshit insane! You don't offer to marry someone after they dump you!"

"I really think you should consider it, Mia. Demetri would be able to provide well for you. He's on the fast track to management, and with it a year-round job at the resort. What are you going to do to support yourself in the summer? You can't just live with us forever."

"I'll get a job. I'll figure something out! I'm not going to marry someone just because they're willing to put a roof over my head!"

"Mia, calm down and think rationally."

"Rationally?" Mia stood up, leaning over the desk and shouting at her father. "Rationally? I'm an adult now! The rational thing to do is to let your daughter date whoever she damn well pleases! This the twenty-first century, and I don't need your permission to live my own life!" With that she stormed out the door.

"Mia! Listen to me; you're making a huge mistake!" But Mia was gone, leaving only the unopened bottle on his desk. The hamster smiled at George, but George did not smile back. Frustrated, he looked back down at his spreadsheet and tried to figure out who he would need to stay for the late group lesson line-up today.

# 5:00 PM

# Lesson Meeting Area

There is a common myth that the Eskimos have many words for snow. This is ridiculous largely because there is no Eskimo language; there are a large number of different but similar languages spoken by various groups of Inuit people. In reality, they do not have many words for snow, but their languages allow adjectives to be combined freely with words. The languages are polysynthetic, meaning that a "word" can be an object, or a phrase, or even an entire sentence. To an outsider, it sounds as if they have many different words, but to an Eskimo it is just a few words that can be combined with many modifiers.

There is another myth, common among those who want to debunk the idea that Eskimos have many words for snow, in which it is claimed that the Eskimo languages have the same number of words for snow as the English language does. People who make this claim have clearly never spent much time in the company of serious skiers.

Skiers have hundreds of words for snow, possibly thousands, because snow exists in thousands of different forms. There are fifteen known solid phases of water. Snowflakes themselves exist in infinite variety, consisting of all shapes and sizes. Variables such as water content, temperature, boundary layers, contaminants, and much more produce a wild variety of snow that can be seen on snow covered mountains around the globe.

Many of these names are simply descriptive. Ice, dry snow, and wind crust are all fairly intuitive. A large number of the names come from foods the snow resembles, such as mashed potatoes, sugar, and corn. Some are foreign words that reflect skiing's European roots, such as firnspiegel, graupel, and sastrugi. The best words are strange enough that non-skiers will believe you are making terms up, such as wet duck feathers, upside-down snow, and death cookies.

Skiers need these words to describe the wild varieties of snow, which can change substantially around a mountain. There may be white gold in the trees that turns to glop where gaps allow the sun to hit it, or perhaps creamed corn in the middle of a run that changes to slud, a nasty mix of snow and mud, near the edges. And every good skier understands the sun clock, or the effect of the time of day on the conditions of the snow.

Typically snow will be hard enough to walk on

in the early morning, frozen by the extreme cold of a mountain night. During the morning it will soften, until at some point it becomes water-logged and mushy. This will continue until the sun sets, at which point it rapidly refreezes and becomes icy. But while this is a typical cycle, it is by no means the only one possible.

After a large cold front drops a large amount of dry snow, there may not be enough water content in the snow to melt and freeze. Instead, the sun causes sublimation, where snow transitions directly from a solid to water vapor, without ever becoming a liquid. As a result the sunset does not ice up the powder, but leaves it soft and inviting. Today's storm was one such event, and while instructors might normally have been trying to sneak out as the sun went down, today they were all trying to squeeze more skiing into the already busy day.

Generally few students wanted lessons during the five o'clock lineup, and only a few instructors would be made available for it. Between the excellent snow and the festival, today's lineup was crowded, and even private instructors had been asked to assist with the evening group lessons.

Right now Goblin was hiding in the back of the crowd. The on-snow supervisor worked grouping students and matching them to available instructors, and Goblin had no desire to be stuck with a large group of beginners. He stood next to Ron, hiding behind some of the taller instructors.

"Hey, Ron, what's going on?" It had been a busy day, and this was the first time the two had seen each other since the morning meeting.

"Busy day. I got to hit some sweet stuff at lunch. If I can get out of this without any more work, I plan to hit the glades on the backside. You up for it?"

"Yeah, that'd be cool, man." Goblin ran his glove through his mohawk, removing a few clumps of snow that had collected. "Hey, what's up with Anna? She pissed at you or something?"

Ron looked surprised. "What? Why would you say that?"

"I dunno. I just asked her where you were a few hours ago, and she stormed off in a huff. Thought maybe you two had a fight or summin'."

"Oh, right, yeah. The girl's infatuated with her damn snowboard she won. It's wrong for her, but she won't get off it. Damn near killed her on Knife's Edge, and she got pissed at me." Ron paused for a second. "I really wish I could think of a way to get her onto a board more her size."

"Have you offered to buy it off her?"

"Of course I have, but she's in love with the damn thing!"

"Don't look at me, brother, you know I don't get no luck with the ladies."

Ron laughed. Goblin really never understood why all the older women requested him. He didn't know if Goblin was truly oblivious, or just never thought of anyone over thirty in a sexual manner. Either way, Goblin hadn't had a date in two years.

"Hey, Goblin, you still got the hookups?"

"Huh?" Goblin looked around, but it was clear that nobody was listening to them. "Come on, man, after lineup. Not now."

"Yeah, yeah, no problem."

The supervisor assigned instructors to the groups he had created, and the newly formed lessons shuffled out towards their various teaching areas. He then asked for volunteers to attend the final line-up of the day, for which neither Ron nor Goblin raised their hands. Released from duty, they began skating toward the lift and the backside glades.

On the chairlift, Ron asked again. "So you still got the hookups, or what?"

"Yeah, I got hookups, but I ain't holding now. You got needs?"

"No, I was just thinking. What if we slipped Anna a little something at the party tonight. A roofie or something. Nothing too serious, just enough to make her do something stupid. I could catch her kissing some dude. Or maybe she'd just not remember the party and I could tell her I caught her kissing some dude. Either way, it wouldn't matter. I'd get upset, and she'd give me the board to make up and say she was sorry."

"Man, what is wrong with you? That's so... wrong! What demon crawled inside your head and farted that idea out?"

"Look, can you help me out or not?"

Goblin shrugged. "Can't promise I can do that by tonight, but I'll see what I can do. It's your moral compass, not mine."

Ron chuckled to himself. "If you can, pick up a little extra. I know someone else that deserves a little payback."

Goblin turned to face Ron. "Oh yeah? Who?"

"Demetri."

"Demetri? The poindexter ski instructor?"

"Yeah, that's the one. I caught him treating Helen like shit this morning. Trust me, he deserves it."

Goblin shrugged again and looked forward. "Sure, no problem. Never liked the guy much, but Helen's a good girl. Real friendly."

"Almost to the top. Backside glades?"

"You got it."

The pair lifted the bar and prepared to get off. Their plan agreed on, neither felt any more hesitation about the upcoming night's events.

# 5:30 PM

# Top of Chair Nine

A ski resort doesn't close down when the sun goes down. Sunlight is a precious commodity in a northern winter, and even in the more southern climes it certainly doesn't appear in great quantities in the depths of December. Most resorts illuminated great swaths of the mountain with hundreds of floodlights, ensuring that guests would be able to continue to ski and ride well into the night. Resorts often wouldn't shut down the lifts until ten, or even midnight.

The lift attendants worked rotating shifts to ensure complete coverage, but this being the Snow Festival they had been running more lifts than usual and some of the attendants were putting in extra hours. Once the sun set, this became considerably more painful, as the darkness brought with him his sister, the cold. And the chill of a winter mountaintop rushed in at dusk with surprisingly speed, catching many a beginner completely unawares.

Robin was not caught unaware, but was bundled up tightly at the top of Chair Nine, a fresh cup of coffee to keep him warm. His day was technically over, but Frank had yet to relieve him. From the schedule it looked like Frank had another two hours to go, which made it a very long day for him. Given that, he wasn't surprised that Frank was a little late.

Robin had just come in from rebuilding the offload ramp and was frozen. He kicked the small space heater. He didn't know why they kept it on; it put out less heat than the coffeepot that was in constant use. Realizing there was nothing else to do for warmth, he took a large gulp of his coffee.

The room was just beginning to regain its warmth when Frank opened the door wide. "My faithful hound, I am here to relieve you!"

"And how I am relieved to hear you say that," responded Robin playfully. "I mean, Woof!"

"Anything up?"

Robin ceded his stool to Frank, and passed the sign-in clipboard to him. "Nope. I just rebuilt the ramp for you a few minutes ago."

"Awesome, thanks. Coffee?"

"Fresh pot."

"Awesomer still." Frank glanced down at the board. "Off for the night, then?"

"Yeah. Although I put some lines in for myself

for the play. Mind if I go over them with you so we can see if they work?"

Frank shrugged and tipped the pot into his cup. "Sure, why not?"

Robin pulled out his script, on which he had made numerous additions. "So you know your line that goes 'Shall I hear more, or shall I speak at this?'

Frank did indeed know that line. It was near the beginning, and thus practiced more frequently than the others. "Sure, right after Juliet says she'll renounce her family name."

"Right. Well, I think as your faithful hound, you should ask me, and I'll respond."

"Respond? How? Will you wag your tail at the audience?"

Robin chuckled. "No, I'll bark, as a dog."

"How so? Just say 'bark'?"

"Of course not, you nitwit. I'll bark like this." Robin made a quiet arf.

"They'll never hear that," admonished Frank. "You'll have to use your man voice to be heard at the play. Or, at least in your case, your hound voice. Certainly not your puppy voice; I'd peg you for a pussy rather than a dog."

Robin glared. He'd practiced his bark throughout the day. "Well, how about this?" He let loose a **RUFF** from the diaphragm. "Better?"

"Ah, yes, that's much better. That's the kind of dog I like to hang around with."

"You don't think that will scare the audience?"

"Naw, they'll love it. You'll steal the show."

"I just think that might be a bit much, frighten the ladies. Perhaps I should bark loudly but sweetly, a gentle roar?"

"Let's hear it then."

Robin coughed to clear his throat, a released a very loud, but sweet, **ARF**.

"That sounded as if a very large rabbit were in a lot of pain. I would stick to the woof if I were you."

"I shall practice my arf over the night and see if I cannot improve on it. Shall we continue?"

"By all means."

Robin returned his focus to the script. "So after I speak, you respond with 'Well spoken, my faithful hound! If only I had the courage to do so.'"

Frank was aghast. "No, you can't add lines to me! Just add in your own part. I'm not going to have a two-way discussion with a dog, that's preposterous!"

"But I have a speaking part! You have to talk back to me, or else I'm just comic relief!"

"I'll have no part of speaking to a dog."

"Come on Frank, let's make this work. Here, I'll take out some of them, so you'll only respond a few times." Robin reached for the eraser.

"No, I'll say my lines and you say yours, and that's final."

Robin fumed. He had spent a lot of time working on Frank's new lines. "I'm going to talk to Peter about this!"

"Go right ahead, I don't care."

Robin grabbed his script off the desk and shoved it into his backpack. "Asshole," he exclaimed as he stormed out of the shack.

"Whiny little bitch," muttered Frank.

# 6:15 PM
# Backside Glades

The floodlights illuminated the slopes across all the open runs. Some areas of the mountain were too remote to easily light up, and would be roped off before sunset. The resulting concentration of skiers could make the already crowded slopes near the primary lifts and main lodge more crowded, even as many skiers began heading home.

The glades that ran between runs could not be easily roped off. And although they were not illuminated, they would technically still be open. But nobody in their right mind would ski down a mountain in the dark. Fortunately, instructors are rarely in their right minds.

On a clear night when the moon is full, the sun's lunar reflection is plenty to safely ski down an open slope. In the trees, the canopy blocks most of the moon's light, leaving skiers to navigate in the dark.

If one must ride through trees in the dark, the wise thing to do would be to wear a headlamp. Many of these headlamps project over 200 lumens into the night, which in a tightly focused beam can be comparable to the intensity of a car headlight with its broader focus. It's certainly enough to see all the trees around you.

Goblin and Ron did not wear such headlamps.

Goblin and Ron rode through the glades between runs on the backside of the mountain, using slivers of light weaving through the trees from adjacent runs to show the way. It was dangerous and ill-advised, but also fun.

Goblin stopped at the entrance to a particularly steep, narrow, and dense path through the trees not marked on the map but known locally as Devil's Drop. Ron pulled up behind him. Goblin pointed down the chute. "You ever do the Drop in the Dark?"

"Naw, that's crazy. It'd be pitch dark, won't see shit in those trees."

"Come on, last run of the day. I gotta get outta here if I'm gonna try to pick up your shit before the party."

Ron considered it. It was a fun run, and he'd just about had it memorized. But he could see the entrance was already heavily tracked, meaning there was unlikely much soft powder inside. Combined with the low light, it just didn't seem attractive compared to smooth turns in the open glades.

"No, I'm going make my last run down just this side of Speed Demon, see if there's any virgin left out there."

"Suit yourself, man, but I'm dropping this shit. Catch you later!" Goblin hopped into the air and pointed his board into the trees. Within seconds he had vanished from sight.

Ron shuffled himself into a traverse and continued cutting across the slope. The glades had gotten fairly tracked up, and there were areas where the darkness and choppy snow made navigation difficult. He certainly didn't want to push himself into anything darker.

After a hundred yards, he felt something hard hit his ankle and he came to a rapid stop, nearly falling down in the process. He realized he'd hit a log buried by the snow, and thanked his lucky stars that he'd hit it in a slow traverse rather than riding full speed down the mountain. He tried backing it, but his board was lodged firmly in the tree.

"Buggerit," he mumbled, unzipping his pocket to pull out his cellphone. "This fuckin' sucks."

He turned on the cellphone to light up the ground around him. With his other hand, he started digging down to see what was holding him in place. The snow was light, and within seconds he had revealed the log and brushed out a path to back up. He pushed against the log and inched uphill, freeing himself from the trap. And then the cellphone screen timed out, pitching him back into darkness again.

"Fuckin' hell," he muttered, trying to turn the screen back on while holding it in his gloved hand. It wasn't working. Frustrated, he let go of the log and passed the phone into his other hand. He immediately realized his mistake as he began sliding back toward the fallen timber. Instinctively, he rotated the board to face the other direction. The nose scraped against the bark, and he fell face first down the hill into the soft powder.

Ron spat out the snow that had flown into his mouth. "Damn it all to hell."

He quickly righted himself and sat up in the snow. "Where the fuck's my phone?" Gloved hands swept through the snow on each side of him, each pass a few inches deeper than the previous one, but to no avail. If only someone would call him right now... Ron knew if he left this spot he would never find his phone again, but he had no idea how he could possibly find a phone in loose powder in unlit woods at night.

For fifteen minutes he tore up the virgin snow, carefully sifting through every handful of snow in a ten foot by ten foot box around where he had fallen. Did he drop the phone? Did it fly out of his hand? He couldn't remember.

With a final admonishment of "Damn it all to

hell," he eventually strapped his board back on and headed down the back side one last time. He took the well-lit groomed run on the frontside back to the locker room, without his phone.

# 7:30 PM

# Resort President's Office

Theo Riga's office no longer sang the gentle sound of snow falling, but instead reveberated with the dull bass from the main stage. He didn't care for the "loud racket," as he called it, and preferred the melodic tones of a banjo to the harsh chords of an electric guitar. Still, he wouldn't have complained at all if it weren't for the damn bass that reverberated through his office. Nobody used a bass drum in a bluegrass band.

Theo popped an aspirin and returned to his computer. Three quarters of the employees didn't have computer accounts at the resort, but a surprisingly large percentage of his time was still spent on e-mail. The ski resort had a very flat structure; front-line workers reported to supervisors, who reported to directors, who reported to Theo. These reports came in consistently throughout the day via e-mail, often with questions attached. Near the end of the day, each of the directors would usually pop their head in to say hello. This wasn't a requirement of Theo's, but everyone enjoyed his company, so it had grown to somewhat of a tradition. Normally by this time all the directors would have seen him, but it was the Snow Festival, and everyone was busier than normal. He hadn't even seen Lita since sometime before lunch, and it was looking like a long late night in the office.

Theo was looking over the day's numbers for lift ticket sales. Sales were up, both for day passes and season passes. Season pass sales generally dropped by this late in the year, but the weak early season had kept a lot of people from committing for the season. With last night's dump on the ground and more in the forecast, the counters were full of skiers wanting to get their pictures taken, and the day's numbers were looking to be the best of the year so far. Theo started to pull up the previous year's data for comparison when there was a knock at his door.

"Come in," he said, without looking up from his computer.

George Markos walked in the office and shut the door behind him. "Hey, Theo, busy day eh?"

"You got that right. Between the Snow Festival and the, well, snow, this year's pretty close to getting back on track."

"I'll get you the lesson numbers first thing in the morning. We're running extra night lessons for the festival, and I won't have final numbers until then. But

I'd wager we're running about the same as the Snow Festival last year, maybe a little ahead."

Theo looked up from his computer. "That's great, George. How about the new Bring-A-Buddy program, is that doing well?"

Bring-A-Buddy was one of George's new ideas this year. Many skiers would bring friends to the mountain and try to teach them to ski, and this often resulted in a bad experience for the new skier, or at worst, a serious injury. George wanted to divert these potential disasters into the ski school, so he convinced Theo to launch Bring-A-Buddy. Each season passholder could bring a friend once, and the friend would be entitled to a free lift ticket and equipment rental, as well as a private lesson. The season passholder would take the lesson with his friend. At first glance it appeared to be giving away for free what is normally an expensive package, but George and Theo both recognized it as an opportunity to get new skiers interested in the sport – and an opportunity to reacquaint old skiers with the value of continued education.

"It's really picked up. You know the numbers were real low, but it looks like they were just waiting for the snow to fall before bringing their friends out."

"That's good to hear, George. Make sure you let Lita know; she's really interested in that program. I think she's planning to do a bit on it at the Ski Resort Conference this spring."

"Really? That'd be great." Ski resorts were in competition with each other, of course, but when it came to recruiting new customers, they were all on the same team. To Theo it didn't matter which resort convinced someone to take up the sport; once they were addicted to snow sports, they were customers. If he had his way, he would help every resort in the country build better programs for enticing new athletes into the game.

"Hey, George, have you figured out that mess with Mia yet?"

George slumped down into the chair opposite Theo. "No, not at all. I talked to her again, and she won't listen to me. I don't know what to do."

"Lita was pretty mad at me last night, and we talked about it this morning. She's got some good points." George made a face that indicated he doubted the points were that good. "Look, George, I agree with you. But I'm an old man, and times are changing. We aren't in Greece anymore. Mia is a grown woman, and she's got to be able to go out and make her own mistakes."

"But I don't have to put a roof over her head and write her paycheck every two weeks if she won't follow my rules!"

"No, you don't. But, on the other hand, you know damn well she's one of your best instructors." George reluctantly nodded. "She should be; she has a great mentor." Theo reached into the drawer and pulled out the whiskey, shaking it in the time-honored motion of an offer.

"No, thanks, I've still got a lot of work to do tonight. Late hours for the festival."

Theo returned the whiskey bottle. "No problem. It's here whenever you're finished. I doubt I'll leave anytime soon either." Theo paused and took a deep breath. "Look, I'm not telling you what to do. If I were in your shoes, I'd probably be doing the same thing you're doing, and Lita would be chewing my ass out as we speak. All I'm saying is that maybe I'm just a little old-fashioned to be giving you advice on this issue, and maybe my views aren't the... right ones for today's day and age. Maybe it's time to let the young'uns do what they will."

"I don't know, Theo. She's my daughter, I just want the best for her."

"I know, George, I know. But she's got to learn the lessons of an American woman, not an Athenian woman." There was a moment of silence, and it was clear that George had no response. "Just think about it, yes?"

"Alright, I'll think about it."

"That's all I ask." Theo perked up, the serious

tone quickly evaporating from his voice. "Got anything else?"

"No, that's all. Just wanted to poke my head in before I got too busy on the day's reports and lost track of time."

Theo looked back at his monitor. His screensaver had engaged, and he began typing his password to unlock it. "Alright, I'll catch you around. If you're still here when I finally get free of this blasted machine, maybe I'll try to get you up to the Double Black."

"I don't think that'd be a good idea. It's going to be pretty loud in there tonight." George stood up and started toward the door.

Theo chuckled. "Maybe a brandy at my place, then."

"Sounds good, Theo."

# 8:15 PM

# The Double Black Bar and Grill

Après-ski is literally French for "after skiing". In Europe, it refers to the practice of going out and socializing, drinking, and carousing after a day of skiing. In many places this is done while still wearing ski gear, while in other resorts most bars will require a change of attire. In America, the term often refers more generally to ski culture and the skiing lifestyle. The term can also be used pejoratively to refer to people more interested in the culture of skiing rather than the act itself.

Although the exact use of the word may be in dispute, and the manner in which it is conducted certainly varies, the basic concept is universal. Whether a ski resort has two lifts or two hundred, at the end of the day there will be skiers congregated together to consume alcohol. It might be inspired by tradition, or cheesy movies from the 1980's, but more likely it is a natural result of the adrenaline that builds in the system during a day of skiing.

David Fehrety famously said, referring to critics of Olympic skier Bode Miller's penchant for partying, "Apparently, a person who dives headfirst down an icy cliff wearing a spandex jumpsuit is supposed to celebrate with a nice glass of tea." Surprisingly, evening tea sales in ski resort bars remain low.

Like many insular activities, there exist common bonds between all snow sports enthusiasts. The shared love of sliding on snow transcends differences that ordinary people would find too difficult to overcome. Rich and poor, snowboarder or skier, redneck or urbanite, all the denizens of the mountain convene in the same bars and drink together. A man who would turn his nose up at a twenty dollar bottle of wine will happily chug a Pabst Blue Ribbon while sharing tales of exploits with a man wearing a ripped Megadeth tee and a mullet, because for at least as long as the winter blesses them, these men are brothers.

Plus, drinking beer and partying all night is fun.

While European après-ski may begin immediately after the last run, Americans usually take the time to retire to their hotel rooms, shower and change, and eat dinner somewhere out in town. Only after ten or so do the bars start picking up, and they will continue to rage until whenever the local authorities have declared as the final hour at which they will permit anyone to enjoy themselves, also known as closing time. The ability of a skier to drink heavily until three in the morning yet to be ready for first tracks at seven is legendary, with the only explanation being that powder is one hell of a hangover cure.

Being only nine, the Double Black was still mostly empty. The Angry Sex Puppies would be performing on the main stage at the resort, but everyone in the know already knew they were doing another unadvertised show here at midnight. The main stage had all the day guests while the real party would be here, hours later.

And while most of the visitors to Ridge Mountain Ski Resort would eat at the various high end restaurants before going to the bars, Alex knew that on a cold day nothing would beat the Double Black's chili bowl. It was a meal in itself, topped with a heavy layer of jalapeños, selling for just a few cents under six dollars. For a young instructor, it was much more appealing than a thirty-five dollar fillet from the steakhouse next door.

It had been a busy day, and Alex was particularly hungry. For two extra dollars he had a side of fries, which he would dip into the bowl one at a time. With the beer his total came to twelve dollars, less than a single tip. It wasn't luxury, but it beat emptying ketchup packets onto saltines. The only real downside was he was alone at the bar, except for a small group of foreigners huddled in the far corner.

Alex was not alone in his knowledge of cheap

good food, and Demetri walked in to see Alex situated at the end of the bar. Neither had changed out of their school uniforms, preferring to flaunt their ski instructor status. If nothing else, if they were recognized by any students at the bar they would usually get a free round out of it.

Demetri was in no mood to spar with Alex again today, so he placed an order for beef tips at the bar and huddled himself away in a small side booth. He decided he would eat his dinner while studying for his upcoming technical knowledge exam for the next level of ski instructor certification, and socialize after more of the instructors had arrived. He removed his jacket and pulled out his notes while waiting for his meal to cook.

It took only a few minutes for the food to come, and Demetri set down his index cards and dug in. It was difficult reading the cards in the low light of the bar, and Demetri had begun to regret picking the secluded booth. It was private, but that also meant darker. At least with his food in front of him, he could eat without having to feel guilty about not studying. He looked over at the bar to see if anyone else had arrived, but all he saw were the foreigners. Even Alex had left, apparently to use the restroom as he had left a significant amount of fries and half a beer on the bar.

Goblin walked in just as Demetri looked back toward the bar. He was trying to find Ron, but Ron hadn't been answering any of his texts. Goblin figured he would show up at the Double Black sooner or later.

He walked up to the bar.

"Hey keep, you seen Ron around?"

The bartender's name was Sam, and he didn't appreciate being called "keep." Still, everyone in town knew Goblin, and if you knew Goblin you knew it was pointless to ask him to be polite. You might as well try to tell ice to stop being slippery. "Nope. What can I get ya?"

"Shot of Ullr." Goblin put a five dollar bill on the bar, and Sam turned to pour the drink. This was a peppermint cinnamon schnapps popular with the instructors, but virtually untouched by anyone else. Ullr was an ancient Norse god, largely forgotten by time. A few surviving images invariably depict him on skis with a hunting bow, which has led to a popularization in ski towns of *Ullr, God of Snow*. Whether he ever was a god of snow or winter we may never know, but the schnapps proved popular with the instructors.

Goblin downed the shot, and turned to Sam. "Seen Ron around?" Sam shook his head. "What about Demetri?"

"Yeah, he's eating over there." Sam crooked his head toward where Demetri was sitting in the dark. Goblin saw Alex's half eaten meal and mistook it for Demetri's.

"Thanks, man. Keep the change." Sam put

the dollar into the tip jar while Goblin walked along the bar. With one hand in his jacket pocket, he opened a plastic bag and pulled out of a pinch of powder. With a smooth motion he dropped the powder into the half full beer glass as he walked by. Unless someone were watching carefully, they wouldn't have seen anything untoward. Without breaking stride Goblin walked out the side door into the alley, and continued his search for Ron.

One down, one to go.

# 9:15 PM
# Ridge Mountain Ski Resort
# Main Stage

It was cold.

It was cold, but there were fires, and people were huddled around them. There has always been something magical about a cold winter mountain night, and people will flock together to enjoy the bitter cold. In this particular case, they were flocked together to listen to the Angry Sex Puppies, who were miraculously able to play despite the temperature. Large portable heaters were placed at the stage aimed directly at each of the band members.

There are two common and competing theories for how to stay warm on a cold night. The first theory, embraced by science and mothers alike, is to dress warm and stay close to a source of heat. For this reason, hundreds of revelers were pressing as close as they could to the multiple artificial fire pits hosting large natural gas flames. Those who couldn't get close enough to the fire were warmed by the natural body heat of the other revelers.

The second theory, thoroughly debunked by science and detested by all mothers, is that alcohol will warm you up. In this case, the mothers are correct. Alcohol actually is a vasodilator, enlarging the blood vessels near the skin. The result of this is that you will feel warmer, but the body loses heat faster and you become more susceptible to hypothermia. Alcohol and cold weather don't mix.

But it is more fun than just sitting around a fire sober.

Ron looked through the flames at the Angry Sex Puppies. They still hadn't done *Tripping Through the Nosegays*, which he didn't like much anyway. It was too strange and faddish for Ron, but then the band as a whole was a sellout as far as he was concerned. He had mostly come to the concert hoping to run into Goblin, or at least some of the other snowboard instructors. Unfortunately, without his phone he had no way to find them other than walking around town blindly. Eventually they'd all end up at the Double Black, they always did.

The Angry Sex Puppies were singing *Tongs and Bones*, an angry song that bordered on metal. Ron didn't mind it that much; he hadn't heard it before but it wasn't bad. He was considering leaving here and looking for Goblin in some of the bars. It seemed odd that nobody would be here listening to the Puppies, but at least the bars would be warmer. The song ended and there was a moment of quiet. Instead of the normal applause there was a muted roar of mittens thumping together, the sound of a hundred pillows falling onto beds.

"Hey, shit for brains, why aren't you answering your phone?" Ron turned and found himself face to face with Goblin.

"Goblin! I've been looking all over for you! I lost my phone in the glades!"

"Like I said, shit for brains. Gotta keep that zipped up, dude." Goblin laughed at his friend's misfortune. "Hey, I got some stuff like you asked. Don't know much about it, never used it myself, but I've been told it will work. Haven't seen Anna, but I already dropped some in Demetri's beer down at the Double Black while I was looking at you."

Ron nodded. "Cool. It work?"

"It ought to. Like I said, never used it before. Demetri was in the shitter, and I left before he came back."

Ron wasn't a bad guy deep down. He just didn't like the way Demetri had treated Helen. "We ought to check up on him and make sure he's okay. Hate to see the guy get hurt too bad."

Goblin shrugged. "Sure, whatever. These

guys blow."

The pair started walking away from the stage and toward the village. "Damn, it's colder than a witch's titty out here," muttered Ron.

"Hell, I've been out looking all over for you. It's your own damn fault you've been standing outside. If you'd been drinking beer somewhere warm we'd both be feeling good right now."

They reached the road. "Where to?"

Goblin gestured down the road. "A bunch of folks are down at the Horny Moose; Demetri's alone at the Double Black. But around ten-thirty everyone's gonna move there."

The Horny Moose wasn't the real name of the bar. The actual name was The Brown Moose Ski Bar and Lounge. But that was a tongue twister in itself, and the proprietor had hung a giant moose head with gargantuan antlers over the entrance. The antlers were so large they became an attraction in themselves, and the nickname followed naturally.

"Let's check on Demetri first, then we can meet up with everyone at the Moose."

"'Kay."

And with that, the mischievous pair set off back to the Double Black Bar and Grill.

# 9:20 PM

# The Brown Moose
# Ski Bar and Lounge

The Brown Moose Ski Bar and Lounge was a family-friendly bar, at least by ski town standards. It certainly met the bill for a stereotypical ski bar. The walls were exposed wood logs, and the bar itself had an open ceiling with wood rafters. Antique skis and black and white photographs of ski legends decorated the walls, along with a few taxidermic oddities. Besides the oversized moose out front, the owner's second most prized possession was the stuffed jackalope that overlooked the bar.

The moose itself is a very interesting creature. Like the reindeer, moose are large members of the deer family. But words fail to adequately describe the animals, as a moose located in Europe or Asia is more correctly referred to as an elk. However, elk in North America are an entirely different species not related to the moose. Similarly, reindeer and caribou are the same species, except that reindeer exist in Europe and caribou are in America.

To further complicate naming conventions, moose were introduced to New Zealand in 1900. If there was a debate on what to call these animals, it is not recorded, but for the sake of clarity we shall call them moose. They all died off, but ten more were brought into the country in 1910. These too were assumed to have died off, and there has not been a confirmed moose sighting in New Zealand since 1952. In 1972, however, a moose antler was found on the island, spurring theories that there may still be wild moose around. There wasn't another sighting until 2002, when some fur found was DNA tested and shown to belong to a moose. Scientists believe there may be as many as twenty moose in New Zealand, although there are more photographs of the Loch Ness Monster than the Kiwi Moose.

There is also some debate on the correct pluralization of moose. Much like fish, the plural of moose is moose. However, that does not stop the more creative people from inventing words such as mooses, meese, and the ever popular meeses.

Nick, surprisingly, was aware of all of these facts. He was, in his own words, a moose aficionado. He considered it his personal peccadillo, although most others simply considered him weird. He could live with that; weird certainly wasn't the worst thing one could accuse a person of being. For this reason, Nick tended to spend a lot of time in the Brown Moose, as he refused to call it by its more popular nickname.

Tonight Nick was drinking more heavily than usual. It was a festival, after all. And although he had long since come to terms with it, he still would have preferred to play a man, any man, rather than Juliet. Still, it was better than Robin playing a dog.

Nick ordered his third Irish car bomb and gulped it down quickly. An Irish car bomb is essentially a glass of Guinness with a shot of Jameson Irish Whiskey and Bailey's Irish Cream dropped in. Once mixed it must be drank quickly else the resulting mixture curdle. As would be expected, this concoction is not one that should be attempted prior to operating a motor vehicle, utilizing heavy machinery, or attempting intelligent conversation.

Nick looked over the bar and spotted the ski instructor who had assaulted a kid on his lift earlier in the day. He walked over and sat down next to her. "Hey… you're the instructor who jumped over my fence today, aren't you?"

Mia turned and looked at the liftie, who was clearly already drunk. She recognized him. "Yeah, sorry about that. I couldn't let him go up."

"S'okay, no problemo." Nick struggled to avoid slurring his words. "Actually, I was impreshed at how you leapt over the bar so well… Can I buy you a round?"

Mia looked down at her nearly full beer. "No, thanks, I'm good. I suspect you've probably had enough to drink yourself." She paused for a second. "I'm sorry, your name is?"

"Nick. At your service." Nick flagged down the bartender. The instructor was absolutely right, he should slow down. "Hey, Betty, can I just get a PBR?" Take it slow, that was the key.

Mia shook her head. If this place was going to fill up with drunks early, maybe she would head over to the Double Black early.

"Hey, Miss, can you do me a favor?"

Mia groaned silently. She really didn't want to have to talk to this inebriated liftie, but her natural desire to help people intervened. "What do you need?"

"Can you help me rehearsh my play for tomorrow? Sit's *Romeo and Juliet*, and I'ms Juliets."

Mia took a good look at Nick for the first time. "You've got a mustache," she pointed out.

"Yesh, buts it's comedy."

"*Romeo and Juliet* is a tragedy."

"Yesh, but we're funny. We've even got a dog." He waved the script in front of her. "So wilsh you do it?"

Mia looked around. "I'd love to," she started, "but I just saw my friends walk in. Sorry, maybe another time." She grabbed her drink and left the bar to meet Helen and Anna taking off their jackets.

"Mia! How've you been!" Helen gave Mia a friendly hug, spilling some of her beer.

"I'm fine. Just had some drunk liftie at the bar hitting on me, though. Mind if we head over to the Double Black a little early? I really don't want to hang around him."

Anna shrugged. "Sure, do you mind?" Helen shook her head. "What about your beer?"

Mia looked at the nearly full glass. "I'll drink it quick." As if to demonstrate, she took a large gulp.

There was a momentary pause in the conversation, so Helen decided to fill it. "Anna was telling me what a dick Ron's been to her today. He's totally jealous about her dragon snowboard."

Mia lowered the glass briefly. "Really? I thought you two were getting along just fine."

Anna shrugged. "We were, but he's infatuated with that board. Part of me wants to give it to him just so he'll shut up, and part of me wants to ride it in front of him just to piss him off."

"I told her to tell him to suck it," added Helen.

Mia finished her glass and set it on a nearby railing. "Come on girls, let's head over to the Double Black."

## 9:30 PM

## The Double Black Bar and Grill

 

The Double Black Bar and Grill was named for the double-black trail rating. In North America, Australia, and New Zealand, trails are rated into one of four categories. In theory, the ratings are only supposed to be used for comparison within a resort, so a green trail simply means that the trail is easier than most other trails *at that resort*. In practice, however, resorts have realized that trail ratings are an important marketing tool. A resort that wants to appeal to advanced skiers will boast few green trails, whereas a resort that wants to attract beginners will designate many trails as green. It is important to understand that ratings are subjective, and depend greatly on weather, conditions, and the marketing gurus at any given resort. Having said that, there are rough generalizations that can be used to understand trail difficulty.

Green circles are used to indicate easy slopes. Not all green trails are suitable for complete beginners, but green trails are unlikely to result in high speeds or major injuries. A green trail will be groomed, wide enough that a person who has difficulty turning won't immediately be flung off into the woods, and generally flat enough that falls will hurt pride more than bones.

Blue squares are used to indicate intermediate slopes. These slopes will usually be groomed, and generally make up the majority of a ski resort. Blue slopes run a wide range of different configurations, but are generally steep enough that an out of control skier could be seriously injured. Fortunately, the majority of skiers are skillful enough to ride these slopes safely.

Black diamonds represent advanced slopes. A black diamond slope will generally have something that makes successful navigation more difficult and requires a specific skill. The slope may be moguled, or contain deep powder, extreme steepness, or trees that must be dodged. Like blue slopes, black diamonds have the potential for injury if a mistake is made. And like blue slopes, the majority of skiers believe they are skillful enough to ride these safely. Unfortunately, many of these skiers are wrong.

Double black diamonds represent expert-only trails, where a failure in the skier's judgment could mean serious injury or worse. These may be steep enough to result in uncontrollable falls, contain cliffs, very narrow trails, or other obstacles designed to brown the skiers' trousers. Universally recognized as fun, these trails are usually not very crowded, as even the most overconfident intermediate skier will only make the mistake of attempting these once. Most double black trails are difficult enough that even walking on them can be extremely hazardous.

Virtually every resort has a fifth category, that of the unmarked trail. Unmarked trails are intentionally left off the trail map specifically to prevent visitors to the resort from finding them. These are trails so nether-lip-puckeringly difficult that the resort would face legal liability if they admitted they existed. Instead, they pretend they aren't there, but turn a blind eye to the locals giving them names and running up and down them. If you think you're ready for these, the best way to find one is to buy a beer or two for a ski instructor or ski patroller in a bar, then politely ask if he could share a few of the best stashes with you. And if he tells you that you aren't ready for it, you should accept his advice and go back to the marked runs without questioning his judgment. Your insurance company will thank you for it.

The Double Black Bar and Grill therefore gets its name from the most difficult of the official trail ratings. By no means a dive, it could get a little wild. By eleven o'clock it was generally crowded, seven days a week. It had an exemption to serve alcohol until two in the morning, a full hour later than the other bars in the village. In short, it was *the* happening place late at night.

By the time Ron and Goblin walked in, it was already getting fairly full. It would be another two and a half hours before the Angry Sex Puppies would play here, but there was a local cover band on the stage, and the bar was no longer empty. There were a number of instructors milling about drinking beer, but Ron focused immediately on Demetri who was now standing off to the side by himself. He nudged Goblin then made for him.

Ron came up from behind and put his arm around him. "Demetri, how's it going?"

Demetri turned. "Oh, fine. This band isn't bad, but I'm waiting for the later shows... You seen Mia around?"

"Nope. Goblin and I just got here, isn't that right?"

"Yeah, haven't been here all night."

Demetri took the last drink of his beer, and shook his head. "Hey guys, I hate to be rude, but I really need to use the john. I'll be back in a few, okay?"

"No problem, we'll be here."

As Demetri walked away, Ron turned to glare a Goblin. "What the fuck was that? I thought you said you slipped him a mickey or whatever?"

"I did, I swear I did! I put it in his drink while he was in the bathroom."

"Did you use enough?"

"How the hell should I know? I've never used this shit before. The guy said a pinch will do!" Goblin took out the bag, intending to demonstrate the dosage.

"Gimme that," Ron said grabbing it out of his hand. "I'll do this myself. Wait here."

Goblin watched as Ron walked over to the bar and ordered three beers. He couldn't see Ron spike any of the glasses, and he eyed them suspiciously when he returned.

"Which one is mine?"

Ron took a sip from his beer. "That one," he indicated. "The other one is for Demetri."

Goblin cocked an eyebrow. "You sure? I don't wanna get fucked up tonight."

"Yeah, man, trust me."

Goblin grabbed the glass, and carefully took a small sip. It tasted like beer.

Demetri returned from the bar to find his glass had magically refilled. "Thanks, what do I owe you?"

"Don't sweat it. Everyone deserves a round on a powder day, enjoy."

Demetri shrugged and took a swig of his drink. He didn't see Helen, Mia, and Anna enter the bar from the side door.

"Oh, God, it's Ron," exclaimed Anna. "I don't want to talk to him right now."

Helen tugged her over to the booths, where they

would be partially hidden in the darkness. "It's okay, we'll hang out over here; he won't see us."

Anna resisted. "Okay, I'll meet you there in a second. I gotta use the ladies' room first."

Mia followed Anna. "I'll go with you."

"No problem, I'll save your seats."

Helen slid into the darkened booth, not noticing that it was occupied. It was only as Helen put her jacket on top of what she assumed was a pile of other patrons' jackets that she realized the pile was breathing. She removed her jacket from his face and leaned in.

"Alex?"

Alex heard his name and opened his eyes. "Helen?"

"Are you drunk? It's only like nine thirty!"

"Huh? No, I don't think so... I'm just a bit tired, that's all." His appearance indicated differently. He looked at Helen. She was leaning over to see him in the dark, and her ample cleavage bounced tauntingly just inches from his face. "God, you're beautiful."

"What?" Helen immediately sat up straight. "What did you say?"

Alex sat upright, his head much clearer than before. "I said you're beautiful. I've never really noticed before, but you really are." He reached up and brushed her hair behind her ear. "Your eyes are amazing."

Helen scooched down the booth seat a few inches. "You're scaring me, Alex. You're dating Mia."

Alex reached out and put his hand on Helen's. "I don't care about Mia. I want you, Helen!"

"Alex, you're drunk, and I'm leaving." She grabbed her jacket and headed out the booth. She was halfway down the street before she heard Alex's voice behind her, shouting her name. She picked up her pace, trying to get away from him, but could hear him following behind.

Helen's mind reeled, and she shook not just from the cold, but also emotion. She would never do anything to come between Mia and Alex. Why would he do this to her?

## 9:45 PM

## North Main Street

Mid-evening is a special time of night on the streets of a ski town. In the morning, there is a tension between the expectation of joyous ski runs tempered by the early morning grogginess. In the early evening, the streets are full of skiers who are sore and hungry. Late at night there will be many young drunk men, doing the best they can to avoid vomiting until they return to their hotel rooms. But at this special time of night there is only the anticipation of great times ahead, and the people on the streets are universally happy.

The cold dry air does little to attenuate sound, and the giggles of women walking to the bars reverberates off the buildings. Ice on the streets amplifies the sounds further, and laughter can be heard throughout the village. It is a magical time where all are happy.

Nick was not happy. He was doing his best not to puke in the alleyway, clearly several hours ahead of schedule for alcohol consumption. He was well into the "why did I ever do this?" phase of inebriation, with a few thoughts of "why didn't I eat dinner before drinking?" He managed to suppress his bile and decided maybe it was better that he hadn't eaten. He leaned against the wall and waited for his condition to either improve or worsen, without any clear idea of which would come first.

Helen stole a glance behind her and saw that Alex hadn't rounded the corner yet. She ducked into the alley to hide. Slowly and quietly, she backed along the wall keeping her eyes on the entrance. Her back pressed against something warm and soft, and she realized she was not alone in the dark alley.

Quickly, Helen moved behind the stranger to better hide her from her pursuer. She saw Alex walk into the alley and look in her direction. Panicked, she grabbed the stranger and began kissing him, hiding herself in her temporary lover's arms. The smell, and taste, was atrocious, and she realized whoever she was kissing had been drinking far too much.

Nick was dumbfounded, and realized he must be dreaming. He decided to go along for the ride, returning the kiss and embrace with all the energy he was capable of mustering. He wrapped his arms around her body, or at least what he assumed was her body, and pressed her close to him.

Alex saw the shapes in the dark alley and squinted. They were clearly two people in love, ignoring him. Frustrated, he continued down the street looking for Helen.

Helen pushed the stranger off her. "Um, sorry about that. I was hiding from someone."

Nick hiccupped a hiccup that he had been suppressing throughout the kiss. He blinked a few times, then looked at his suitor. "Helen?"

"Oh, dear God."

"Helen, isch thatcho?"

Helen looked at the face. It looked familiar, and he clearly knew her name. A student? Worse, another instructor?

"Itsh me, Nick!"

Helen mentally reduced the number of people she might have kissed down to just those named Nick, but still couldn't place the face in front of her.

"Nick, the lifsch attendant? We seesh eatsother every day on the schlopes!"

"Nick!" Helen certainly saw Nick every day, but she couldn't remember ever saying more than "Good morning" to him. She didn't know his name, and knew that he never would have known hers if she didn't have it plastered on her uniform. She then corrected herself, and *hoped* that he never would have known her name if she didn't have it plastered on her uniform. She was in no mood for meeting new people, and began searching for an excuse to leave.

"Look, about that kiss... I was trying to hide from a guy who's been chasing me, that's all. I didn't mean anything by it, I'm sorry."

"Hey, itsch all right. I'm happy to he-" Nick was cut off as he expelled his last beer onto the pavement.

"Oh, God. Are you alright?"

Nick held on to the wall, and when that failed to support him, he began holding onto the ground for support. "I'll be fine, don't worry." He began to look around for a nice place to lie down.

Helen looked around in the alley. It was cold, and Nick could be seriously injured sleeping unprotected out here. On the other hand, she really didn't want to be with anyone else right now, and carrying a loud drunk person around only multiplied the odds that Alex would be able to find her. Her better nature won out, and she played the Samaritan.

"It's freezing out here. Let me at least walk you to someplace warm."

"Sursech..."

Helen assumed that meant yes, and dragging Nick's arm over his shoulder, began working her way back to the Double Black. Normally it would have only taken a minute or two to get there, but Nick was heavy and not helping much.

Halfway down the street, Nick stopped to puke in a planter. Helen held him patiently, shivering in the cold.

"Helin, yousch scho nisch to me...." Nick looked up at her. "Yoursch pretty, schtoo."

"Oh, God, not you too." Helen hoisted him back up to a walking position. "Don't you get started now."

# 10:00 PM

# The Double Black Bar and Grill

The job of Public Relations Director is critical to any ski resort. Only a quarter of Americans engage in any winter physical activities at all, and only about half of those do any skiing or snowboarding. Every resort has to work hard to get new skiers and riders onto the slopes, or the entire industry will melt away into an eternal summer.

Beyond the basic economics, there is an image problem for snow sports with roots that go back decades. To many people, skiing is a rich person's pastime, akin to yachting or polo. Ordinary people can't afford these frivolous indulgences, and spend their winters at home drinking beer and watching football.

Certainly some resorts have done little to rectify this situation. High end destination resorts push an image of exclusivity while charging patrons thousands of dollars for luxurious slopeside accommodations. Sushi bars and wine tasting rooms have sprung up on the streets of many resort towns, and certainly prices have risen accordingly.

But this reveals the heart of the image problem. Resorts want to soak the rich who are willing to throw away large sums of money to live the lavish lifestyle, but they recognize the need to cater to ordinary middle class Americans. This has created a sort of dual pricing structure. For many resorts, the cost of an annual season pass is often the same as about ten days of skiing. Five star hotels are often a block away from a hostel with low-cost bunkbeds. And while a pair of good skis can cost upwards of a thousand dollars, knowledgeable customers will often know how to obtain the same pair on sale for less than half price.

The Public Relations Director is therefore forced to walk a thin line, neither alienating the wealthy who are looking for exclusivity nor scaring off the core customer base who worry about the expense of skiing. Like a politician seeking election, they must segment the market and deliver the most appropriate message to each target audience.

Tonight Phil was targeting his message to the crowd in the Double Black Bar and Grill.

Phil stood on the stage, still wearing ski pants and a resort jacket. He was thanking the nameless local cover band for their performance, and trying to inject some praise for the resort before introducing the next band to take the stage. It was easy to talk up the resort when the snow was soft and deep, more difficult in the lean years. Like many in a ski town, the fickle whims of Mother Nature had a lot to do with his job performance. He concluded his pitch for everyone to come back again next weekend, and moved on.

"...and without further ado, let's give a grand Ridge Mountain Resort welcome to..." Phil looked at his palm. Under the hot lights, his sweat had melted the name. He decided to give it his best shot. "Ummm... Welcome to Devilish-Holy Fray!" He exited stage right to polite applause.

The lead singer stepped up to the microphone. "We're Devil's Holy Day from Denver, and this is *Truth Kills Truth!*" The drummer began counting aloud, and by the count of four hard rock was once again filling the bar.

Phil walked up to the bar and ordered another Coke. He was on duty, and he never drank alcohol on duty. He looked at the purple-mohawked and metal-pierced man next to him. "Cheers!" he said, raising his glass.

Goblin peered at the somewhat familiar man next to him. Who would drink soda at this hour in the Double Black? "Whatever, dude."

Helen leaned Nick against the bar on the other side from Phil. "Hey Goblin, have you seen Alex?"

Goblin shook his head. "Haven't seen him all night."

Nick hiccupped loudly, and Phil looked over. "It looks like he's had enough. Perhaps you should take him home?"

Helen sighed. "He's not with me. I just found him outside and brought him in to warm up." She looked at Goblin. "He's one of the lifties, you don't happen to know where his friends are, do you?"

Goblin shook his head again, but Phil lit up. He suddenly recognized the pair as instructors from the school. "You two need to take care of him and get him somewhere safe. We can't let employees go around drunk potentially hurting themselves or someone else."

Goblin had "taken care" of drunken friends many times before. He downed the last of his beer and slipped his arm through Nick's armpits. "Don't worry, Mister Resort Man, I'll take care of him."

Goblin half-dragged, half-carried Nick through the crowd until spotting a vacant booth in the back. They slid into one side together, and Goblin nestled his head in the back corner of the booth.

Nick was barely conscious. "Hey, thanksch man..." he mumbled before reclosing his eyes.

Goblin smiled a friendly smile. "Just go on off to sleep. Goblin's here to take care of you. I'll make it all better. You sleep tight while I give you your medicine..."

Goblin rummaged through his pockets. All instructors carried a waterproof pen of some sort. Some carried fancy space pens that could write upside-down underwater, while others carried a simple Sharpie that sold for a dollar at the store. Goblin carried a simple Sharpie that had been left unattended in the locker room, and on the third attempt, his fingers located it.

Goblin considered himself a performance artist when it came to drunken friends. Opportunities like this only came around a few times a year, and they needed to be considered carefully before rushing in. The shape of an individual's face, the hair, even the color of the eyes should be weighed into the evaluation. Amateurs might just draw a penis on someone's face, but Goblin was no amateur.

After a few minutes deliberation, he settled on a horror motif to maximize Nick's expansive chin. Using the cheeks and chin area, he carefully outlined a gaping maw, and filled it in with razor sharp teeth. He then filled in the mouth, covering Nick's skin and lips with black. The end result was that with his mouth shut, Nick appeared a monster roaring. The mustache, sitting atop the visage, served to make him look even less human.

Goblin stepped back and admired his handiwork. He reasoned that Nick would learn not to overdo it so early in the evening, and everyone else would get a good laugh. It was a service to humanity.

# 10:20 PM

## The Rigas Residence

Many years ago, ski resort towns were small affairs where the resort workers would live when they weren't at work on the slopes, interspersed with a few hotels and bars for visitors. Over time the dynamic has grown, and more business has meant less room for the workers. The price of real estate in a ski resort town has grown so high that virtually all residential properties are managed timeshares, effectively informal hotels for guests who want a more "comfy" feel to their vacation.

The employees who once lived in the middle of town have been pushed out to the outskirts, or in some cases, even to new satellite towns a few miles down the road. The affordable grocery stores and so forth moved with them, providing necessary services at affordable rates while the tourists were subjected to unreasonable profit margins in the center of town.

Theo Rigas was an exception. He had moved

to Ridge Mountain before the ski town real estate boom, and had remained in the same house the entire time. He had a large beautiful home on Ridge Road, separated from the adjacent buildings by ten feet of snow and a well-maintained white wooden fence. Unique in resort, it was the only building left in the downtown area set back from the sidewalk with a front yard. The back abutted the resort property, and Theo would often use a snowmobile to get to and from his office. The home was a landmark of the town, and could have easily sold for fifteen times his annual salary.

Gentle bluegrass music filled the sitting room where George Markos and Theo Rigas were sipping Scotch and playing cribbage. The pair began playing cards on occasion many years ago, and the Mountain Snow Festival seemed like as good an occasion as any other.

"Fifteen two, fifteen four, and a double run of three for twelve." Theo lifted his rear peg and moved it twelve holes in front of his lead peg. "Looks like we're tied. Your deal." He slid the deck toward George.

George ignored the deck and opted instead to pick up his Scotch. "This will have to be the last game for me; tomorrow will be another busy day and I'll need to get an early start." Theo nodded as George picked up the deck of cards and shuffled in silence.

When both players had been dealt six cards, Theo spoke without looking up from his hand. "Have you had an opportunity to think about our last conversation?"

George put two cards down beside the board. "Hm?"

"Your daughter." Theo placed two cards on top of George's and cut the deck.

George flipped over the top card, revealing a jack of hearts. "Heels," he said, scoring two points for himself. "No, sorry, Theo; I've been pretty busy all day."

Theo nodded. The pair began pegging, playing cards one after another, until both had played their entire hands.

George picked up his hand and waited for Theo to score his points. "Is Lita on your case about this?"

Theo spread his cards out on the table. "Fifteen two, fifteen four, fifteen six, fifteen eight, and a pair royal for fourteen. Right into the stink hole." He moved his peg accordingly. "A little. But I do care for you both, and I'd like to see Mia back here next season. I've seen her teach; she's quite good with the kids."

George laid down his hand. "Triple run of three for fifteen." He picked up the crib and laid the cards out. "And a nineteen point crib. You got lucky there. Looks like we get another hand."

Theo began shuffling the cards. "Do you think Mia will make a career out of skiing?" Hearing no immediate response, he began dealing the cards again.

"I don't know. Perhaps." George picked up his cards and began sorting them. "I don't think she's made up her mind yet."

Theo placed to cards to the side. "What would you prefer she decided?"

George put two cards aside as well, and cut the deck. "I'm not sure."

Theo theatrically flipped over the top card. A jack would have ended the game with a win for him, but instead he revealed a deuce of diamonds. "George, to put it bluntly, I imagine the outcome of this issue will weigh heavily on her decision."

George placed a card face up in front of him. "I hadn't considered that. Two."

Theo scrunched his brow. The game was close, but he had no twos. Playing an ace would prevent George from earning a fifteen, but left open the possibility of losing to a run. He reasoned that George was likely to have thrown away his high cards and opted to play a five. "Seven."

George quickly responded, laying down a queen. "Seventeen."

Theo smiled. "I've won, old friend."

"Don't be too sure of yourself, the game is still on."

Theo placed a king down. "You have no four, or you would have opened with it. Twenty-seven."

"You're quite right." George placed another two on the table. "Twenty-nine."

Theo played his ace. "Thirty. Unless you have an ace you somehow forgot to play?" His hand hovered over the board.

George calmly laid down his remaining two cards. "Go. Well played." He extended his hand in concession.

The pair shook, and George began donning his winter coat. "It's been a pleasure as always."

"Anytime. Please do take some time to think about what you're going to tell Mia when you see her. You'll have to say something to her in the morning; no decision is a decision in itself."

George headed for the door. "You are right again. See you on the slopes?"

Theo laughed. "These old bones? On festival weekend? I'll see you in my office. Be safe."

And with that, George headed out into the night.

# 10:30 PM

# The Double Black Bar and Grill

Skiers are, as it turns out, Parrotheads. Nobody really knows why.

Jimmy Buffett sings about warm summer days on Caribbean beaches, walking barefoot through warm sand while drinking a piña colada. Skiers tromp heavy boots through deep snow in freezing temperatures to drink a PBR in a ski bar. While Jimmy Buffett sings about sleeping until noon, skiers know the best powder is found in the early morning.

Yet every ski bar has a jukebox, and the most worn out tracks are inevitably Buffett's. Maybe it's the shared rejection of society, or perhaps the dream of living the life that most only visit on vacation. Perhaps it's just that the Coral Reefer Band's simplistic stylings are easy for drunken revelers to comprehend. For whatever reason, Jimmy Buffett is popular in ski towns.

The Double Black Bar and Grill was no exception. Although it was a hard rock night, they were playing the jukebox between bands, and *Changes in Latitudes, Changes in Attitudes* was currently playing. The apparent irony was lost on the crowd, who were mostly using the reduced volume of the music to catch up with each other while refilling their drinks.

Anna and Mia were doing exactly that. They'd lost Helen some time ago, and weren't sure where she'd gotten off to. They'd mostly spent the night listening to music and avoiding Ron. So far they had been fairly successful, but their lucky streak ended at the bar.

"Hey, babe," Ron crowed. "Where have you been all night?"

Anna jumped at his voice. "Hanging out with my friends. I just came here for more beer."

"Whatcha drinking? I've got a tab open."

Anna considered. She was still angry at Ron, but this was certainly a step in the right direction to make it up to her. She was on a strict budget, and not having to buy drinks would help her meet it. She decided to test Ron.

"I'm drinking the Breckenridge Vanilla Bean Porter, and Mia's drinking their light lager." She waited for Ron to object to paying for Mia's beer as well, but the objection never came.

"Sure, no problem. Where are you sitting?"

Anna pointed. "Just standing around over there."

"I'll be right over with the drinks, ladies." Ron grinned. For the cost of two beers, he had managed to be alone with Anna's drink, and would have no trouble slipping the last of his drug into her glass.

Anna was somewhat confused, but accepted the generosity. Not only did Ron agree to buy the round, but he wasn't going to make her hang around at the bar waiting for them. It was certainly out of character. She walked back to Mia.

"Where are the drinks?"

"Ron's buying them; he'll bring them over."

Mia raised an eyebrow. "You're speaking again?"

Anna shrugged. "I dunno. He did buy the beer, and he was a perfect gentleman."

Mia put her hands together on the side of her face, and cocked her head to the side. She fluttered her eyelids. "Positively dreamy…"

"Oh, fuck off, Mia. It's free beer."

"There you are!" Helen pulled into the group. "Oh my God, you won't believe what's happened to me!"

"Well, girl, do tell!"

Helen paused. She had decided she was going to tell Mia everything, but standing in front of her now she wasn't so sure. Alex was clearly drunk, and telling Mia what he had done would ruin their relationship. Helen couldn't stand to hurt her friends.

"I, uh, went outside for some fresh air, and, um, kinda accidentally kissed a liftie."

143

Anna made a vulgar *mmmm* noise. "Was he hot? Who was it?"

"I dunno… He was drunk, and it was stupid." Helen's mind raced. She couldn't explain why she had kissed him without explaining why she had left in the first place. She had painted herself into a corner.

"Details, girl, details!" Anna and Mia were insistent.

"Well, it started because he was drunk, and I was helping him walk…" Helen spoke slowly as she tried to find a way to finish the story that didn't make her sound like a silly slut. "We were in an alleyway off Main Street…"

"Here you are, girls." Ron set the drinks on a floor speaker, and began divvying them out. "One light lager for Mia, one porter for Anna, and an IPA for myself… Oh, Helen, I didn't know you were here! Would you like my beer, and I'll go fetch another for myself?"

"No, thanks, I'm okay. I was just about to leave anyway."

"What?" cried Anna. "The story was just getting good, we want to hear it all!"

"Maybe later. I'll catch you around, okay?"

As Helen walked off into the crowd, Anna smacked Ron hard in the ribs.

"Ouch! What was that for?"

Helen ducked and weaved through the partiers, trying desperately to find someone, anyone, who she could confide in. Since she had decided not to tell Mia the truth, she wasn't sure who she could talk to. She debated just calling it an early night when someone bumped into her and knocked her to the ground.

"Hey, watch it..." The clumsy oaf turned around and she recognized him. "Demetri?"

Demetri extended a hand to help her up. "Oh, god, Helen, I'm scho sorry..."

"It's okay, really." Helen rose to her feet and looked at Demetri. "Are you okay? You look a little... lost."

"Yea, maybe a bitsch drunk. But I'm okay, really." Demetri stared at Helen. He lifted his hand and brushed her hair out of her eyes. "I'm schorry, Helen. I never meant to hurt you."

Helen looked around for an excuse to leave. She certainly didn't want to tell Demetri about Alex's behavior. "It's okay, really. You didn't hurt me, I just fell. I'm fine."

Demetri held onto Helen's arm, firmly but gently. "No, Helen, I hurt you. I've been cruel to you because I couldn't shee the beauty inshide you... or the beauty outschide."

Helen stopped. She looked Demetri in the eyes. "Seriously, Demetri, are you okay? What's gotten into you?"

145

"Helen, I..." He paused. "I thinkch I lovesch you."

Helen twisted her arm out of Demetri's grasp. "What the fuck is wrong with you?"

"I'm schorry, Helen. I'm scho schorry..."

"You think this is funny? Are you making fun of me?" Helen's face lit up in realization. "Oh my God, you and Alex are in this together, aren't you?"

Demetri's face contorted in drugged confusion. "Alex?"

"You think it's funny to make fun of me? You're assholes, the both of you! I never want to see either of you again!"

Helen stormed off into the crowd. 'Screw Demetri,' she thought. 'Screw Alex, too.' She hadn't told Mia the truth because she didn't want to hurt their relationship, but now she realized just what a prick Alex really was. If Mia dumped Alex, all the better for Mia.

She quickly worked her way back to Anna and Mia. True, Ron was back there too, but she was so angry she didn't care who else heard what she had to say. She was going to put a stop to this charade once and for all.

Helen rolled up to the group and interrupted Mia mid-sentence. "Mia, Mia, you have to listen to me!"

It was at this point that the jukebox cut out and Phil took the stage, introducing the next band, although with his obligatory spiel about how wonderful Ridge Mountain Ski Resort was. Fortunately for the revelers, the microphone was turned off, and they were spared his speech.

Mia turned to look at Helen. "What's wrong?"

"It's Demetri… and Alex. They've teamed up to make fun of me!"

Mia looked at Helen quizzically. "Helen, I doubt that. Alex isn't like that. Besides, those two don't get along, why would they team up for something like that?"

"I don't know!" Helen was holding back tears, and Mia could see it in her eyes. Meanwhile, Anna was swaying back and forth, and grabbed onto Mia's arm for support.

"Anna, are you okay?" asked Mia.

"Yeah, I think I may have just drank too much too fast. I'm going to use the restroom real quick; I'll be right back." Anna swallowed the last of her beer, and headed toward the back of the bar.

"I'll make sure she's okay," said Ron, moving after Anna.

"Thanks!" Anna turned back to Helen. "Now, tell me exactly what happened. What did they do?"

Whoever was responsible for the sound system made it back to their post and turned on the microphone. Helen's answer was inaudible under Phil's acoustically amplified voice. "...rther ado, Crossways and Floods!" The bar erupted in applause, mostly on the logic that any band coming onto the stage this late must be good.

"What? You'll have to speak up to be heard over the band!"

"I said Alex and Demetri are both pretending to love me! They're making fun of me!"

Mia shook her head. The band had started playing, leading with a loud guitar solo. "No, they're just being nice to you!"

"What?"

"I SAID THEY'RE JUST BEING NICE TO YOU!"

"NO THEY AREN'T!"

"WHAT?"

Helen motioned toward the door, attempting to indicate that it was too loud, and they should go outside. Mia nodded, and finished the last of her beer. The pair walked out the door and into the cold night air, stopping under a light post thirty feet away from the building. They were just far enough away to be free of the smoke, and at least as importantly, the smokers.

"Helen, why would Alex say he loves you? He's my boyfriend; he loves me."

"He's an asshole! He's pretending to love me to make me look stupid in front of everyone!"

"Don't talk about my boyfriend like that! You're lying!"

"Mia, listen to me! I'm telling the truth! Alex told me he loves me!"

"Bullshit! I'm going to go get him and prove you wrong! Wait here!" Mia stormed off into the Double Black.

"Dammit," muttered Helen under her breath. It was cold.

Helen paced back and forth for several minutes. Why were Demetri and Alex both treating her so poorly? Why was Mia not listening to her? The pacing didn't help her anger any, but it did help her feel less cold. Eventually Mia returned, dragging Alex behind her. Alex did not look happy, although he did appear much less drunk than the last time Helen had seen him.

"What's this all about? Why did you drag me out into the cold?"

"Tell Helen you don't love her! You're my boyfriend!"

Alex hesitated. "Mia, I do love Helen." Mia gasped. "I was going to tell you, really I was, but I love Helen."

Helen didn't feel any better for being proven right. "See what I mean? And Demetri is in on it too!"

Mia spun around to face Helen. "What did you do to him?"

Helen was taken aback. "Do to him? Nothing! We didn't do anything! He's crazy!"

"Crazy for you!" cooed Alex.

"You fucking slut! You don't take your friends' boyfriends out from underneath them!" Mia advanced on Helen, but Alex held her back.

"Mia, calm down! She didn't do anything, I swear! It's me... I just realized today that I love Helen with all of my heart."

Mia struggled for several seconds before relenting. Alex let go of her, and she hissed "You bitch" at Helen.

The tears were streaming down Helen's face, stinging her skin in the cold air. "I swear to God, I didn't do this! I don't want Alex; I never have!"

A new voice rang out from the direction of the bar. "Hey, Alexsch, have you scheen Helen?" The group spun to see Demetri walking toward the group, clearly inebriated.

Alex snapped back, "Not now, Demetri, we're busy."

"Helen! I'vsch been looking all oversch for you!"

Helen dropped her head into her hands. "Oh, God."

"Helen! Yousch need to lischen to me! I know nowsch that I wasch wrong to treat you scho mean... I lovesch you! Can yousch ever forgivsch me?"

Alex stepped between Demetri and Helen. "I can't believe I'm hearing this! You've been a complete ass to Helen from the day she met you! You missed your chance, back off!"

Demetri pushed his fingers against Alex's chest, pressing until Alex was forced to take a step back to maintain his balance. "And what bichnisch isch it of yoursch who I date?"

Alex brought himself to a full upright stance. "Mine. I'm in love with Helen."

"Bullschit. You are dating Mia."

"Not anymore, I'm not."

"Alesch, get ouch of my way. I'm talking to Helen, and yoursch going to go back inschide with Mia."

"Like hell I am!"

Demetri raised his fists into a loose approximation of a boxer's stance. "Don't makesch me fight you, Alesch!"

"Demetri, you're drunk. Go away!"

Demetri swung at Alex, missing him by at least a foot. Alex lunged forward, grappling Demetri and pinning his arms against his sides. The two struggled briefly before falling together into the snow.

"Stop it!" Mia pulled the two apart from each

other. "Stop it you two!"

The two boys began picking themselves up. "He started it," Alex helpfully pointed out.

Demetri glared at Alex. "Alright, theresch only one way to schettle thisch. Chinese downhill. Meet at the top of Chair Nine at midnight."

Alex returned the stare. "Done."

There was a deafening quiet over the group. After several seconds of silence, Helen finally spoke.

"Are you two both fucking mental?"

# 11:30 PM
# The Brown Moose
# Ski Bar and Lounge

There is a strong connection between the length of the day and depression. Scientists have many theories, many of which involve melatonin, but the sad fact is we don't know why some people are more depressed during certain seasons. Officially classified as Seasonal Affective Disorder (SAD), it affects only 1.4% of people in Florida, but as many as 9.7% in New Hampshire. It's estimated that over a quarter of Alaskans suffer from it, although being Alaskan, they won't admit it.

The disorder generally strikes people in winter, with artificial light therapy being a common treatment. For many people, however, it runs in reverse. These people crave winter, and relish the cold. While the snowbirds fly south for the winter, the powderbirds fly north.

Mild cases are generally self-treated by becoming nightowls. Sleeping until afternoon and staying out all night can reduce your exposure to sunlight, while putting your prime hours in the cooler night air. But for serious cases, there is no easy solution. Winter up north can be Heaven, but a summer with little darkness is Hell.

Not all hardcore skiers suffer from SAD. Some ski instructors remain in the mountains year round, guiding whitewater rafting trips or mountain biking all summer long. But others will curl up inside homes with the windows blocked out, leaving the air conditioning on full blast, trying to deny the summer outside. The luckier ones will move to New Zealand or South America for a second dose of winter.

Late night in a ski bar brings all types in close proximity. Sun worshippers enjoying a ski vacation, but drinking to offset the pain of the darkness, combined with lovers of the night enjoying their prime environment.

Most of these people were not at the Brown Moose Ski Bar and Lounge, colloquially known as the Horny Moose. Most people were in the Double Black, waiting for the Angry Sex Puppies to play, as they were rumored to do at midnight. Consequentially, the Moose only had a few clueless tourists who were unaware of the Double Black, and a number of lift attendants impaired by a combination of alcohol and marijuana who were practicing for a show the following day.

Peter tapped his beer glass with a pen. "Alright, alright, let's get started with this!"

"Oh, fuck off," said Frank.

"Now, come on, we need to start practicing if we're going to get this done and get any shut eye before the morning!"

"We haven't got Nick. We can't have a bloody rehearsal without Juliet!"

Peter shook his head. "He's a half hour late; we can't wait any longer. I'll play the part of Juliet for the rehearsal."

Frank took a swig of his beer. "Alright, whatever." He stood up and faced the assembled lifties. "He jests at scars that never felt a wound. But, soft! What light through yonder window breaks? It is the East, and Juliet is the sun."

Peter coughed. "West."

"Are you sure?"

"Positive. The sun sets in the East, so it's the West."

Frank shrugged. "West it is, then. Arise, fair sun, and kill the envious moon, who is already sick and pale with grief, that thou made art far more fair than she. Be not her maid, since she is envious, her vestal livery is but sick and green,"

A voice from the back suggested that Peter's livery was certainly sick and green, to much snickering.

"And none but fools do wear it; cast it off. It is my lady, O, it is my love! O, that she knew she were! She speaks yet she says nothing: what of that? Her eye discourses; I will answer it. I am too bold, 'tis not to me she speaks. Two of the fairest stars in all the heaven, having some business, do entreat her eyes to twinkle in their spheres till they return. What if her eyes were there, they in her head?"

Frank paused. "What the hell does that mean, anyway? What if her eyes were there, they in her head? Does she carry them around in her pocket?"

"Just get on with it!"

"Alright, alright... Where was I? The brightness of her cheek would shame those stars, as daylight doth a lamp; her eyes in heaven would through the airy region stream so bright that birds would sing and think it were not night. See, how she leans her cheek upon her hand! O, that I were a glove upon that hand, that I might touch that cheek!"

There was a distinct pause, followed by polite coughing and impolite snickering. Robin gave Peter a firm elbow in the side, which caused him to immediately burst out "Ay!"

Frank continued. "She speaks! O, speak

again, bright angel, for thou art as glorious to this night, being o'er my head as is a winged messenger of heaven unto the white-upturned wondering eyes of mortals that fall back to gaze on him when he bestrides the lazy-pacing clouds and sails upon the bosom of the air. Bit of a run-on sentence, isn't it?"

"We'll leave it as it is. Go on."

"I'm done; it's your turn now."

"Oh, right." Peter looked back down at the script. "O Romeo, Romeo! Where are thou Romeo? Deny thy father and refuse thy name, or, if thou wilt not, be but sworn my love, and I'll no longer be a Capulet."

"Shall I hear more, or shall I speak at this?"

"Arf."

"Nonononono! You must be much louder!"

"I will when we do the play, but I don't want to scare the other patrons of his fine establishment."

"If the patrons of this fine establishment are to be frightened, they shall be frightened of your drunken ways. You'll make an ass of yourself before the night is through, a good arfing shan't make a difference."

Robin reared up and faced Frank. "**ARF!** There, are you happy now?"

"Much better, my faithful hound. Now on!"

Peter resumed his faux girl voice. "Tis but thy name that is my enemy."

"Hold on, I thought we were giving Romeo lines

to talk back to me!"

"We never! I told you I wouldn't allow you to change my lines! Shakespeare is involatile! You cannot besmirch the Bard with crass adaptations!"

"We should strive for equal lines!"

"Equal lines? Fair Verona is no democracy!"

Peter chortled. "Well, shall we ask the Prince for counsel?"

The group laughed, obviously drunk at this point. "And who, pray tell, might our princely savior be today?"

Peter looked around. "We shall ask this kind young man who walks into this establishment as we speak. You, there! Come hither and bless us with your fine counsel!"

Nick stumbled toward Peter. He knew they'd be pissed; he was quite late. It was well after eleven before he awoke from his drunken stupor at the Double Black. He was not prepared for their reaction as he approached, however.

What the drunk lift attendants saw was not their good friend Nick, but a misshapen monster with a gaping maw, and large pointy teeth. Goblin's handiwork had not rubbed off, and to the sauced-up actors he was a frightful apparition.

"Aiiiii! Run for your lives!" The lift attendants scrambled over the table, over chairs, and over each other in their haste to depart to safety. "He'll eat us all for sure!"

Nick stood dumbly among the scattered chairs. "What the fuck was that all about?" he mumbled aloud.

"Hey, you!" The bartender called from behind the bar. "Nick, isn't it? You work with those guys, I know you do. You're going to have to cover their tab!"

Nick sighed and walked toward the bar. It was hard to imagine this day getting much worse. He pulled out his credit card, and ordered himself a shot of Ullr.

The bartender grunted as he measured out the dose. "You've got shit on your face," he said.

Nick mumbled a thanks, and brushed off an imaginary piece of lint. He looked around; this place was dying fast. Swallowing his drink, he signed the receipt, grabbed his card, and decided to head back to the Double Black, where at least there was live music and more people.

# 12:00 AM

# Top of Chair Nine

The Chinese downhill is a mainstay of ski movies. The basic principle is simple: a number of participants start at the top of the mountain, and the first one to reach the bottom wins. There are no other rules. Each participant is welcome to take any path they choose down the slopes, although in reality there is rarely any debate on which is the fastest route.

The number of racers can range from just two up to over a hundred. These larger races create new hazards, as skiers and riders will get in each other's way, and those in the rear risk tripping over those who fall in front of them. A large Chinese downhill certainly is a dangerous affair.

Even with fewer racers, there are many opportunities to become injured in a Chinese downhill. Participants will push and shove each other to induce falls. Comedy movies often show unrealistically dangerous weapons employed, but in reality nobody brings a mace to a Chinese downhill. Ski poles are effective enough at tripping people up, and the goal isn't injury, but simply to get to the bottom first. The anything-goes mentality of the movies is, fortunately, a myth. Generally competitors will quickly space out far enough early in the race, and there will be little to no contact throughout the race.

The tradition of the Chinese downhill has inspired boardercross and skiercross, both officially recognized sports where groups of four race down a narrow course with jumps, ramps, and obstacles. The officially recognized sports do not allow intentional contact between participants, but unintentional bumping remains inevitable given the size of the track.

Of course, no resorts permit Chinese downhills, mostly due to the liability risks. When they do occur, they are often done in remote sections of the resort, or after operating hours. Very rarely, they can be held in the middle of the night.

Demetri and Alex had sobered up significantly on the hour-long hike up the mountain. With proper ski mountaineering gear, a skier can move very quickly uphill, considerably faster than a hiker or snowshoer. Carrying skis and walking, however, is a slow trek under the best of circumstances. The two had not spoken the entire journey up, yet stayed side by side as neither was willing to walk behind the other, lest he be seen as out of shape by the other.

At the summit, they both dropped their skis on the ground, and stepped into them. Demetri was the first to speak. "Start at the lip." The actual summit was fairly flat, and a start there would require skating to the slope to begin the race.

Alex shrugged. "Sure. Are they ready for us?"

"Hold on." Demetri pulled off his gloves and dialed his cellphone. Alex could only hear one side of the conversation, but it was clear that Helen was trying to talk him out of it. The frustration in his voice was evident. Eventually he hung up.

"She won't judge the race."

Alex prodded the snow with his pole. "We don't need a judge."

"What are we racing to?"

Alex peered down the mountain, although he knew the base lodge wasn't visible from the summit. "Anyone else down there?"

"Yeah, just about everyone."

"Call Goblin."

Demetri laughed. Goblin would certainly play along. He dialed his phone, and after a quick conversation, turned back to Alex. "Alright, he's standing in front of the main lodge. First one to touch him wins."

Alex lowered his goggles over his eyes. "Whenever you're ready, chump."

Demetri adjusted his pole straps and plotted his line down the mountain. He wordlessly surveyed the dark slope beneath him, debating the quickest route down. After nearly a minute of silence, he simply said "Go," and took off suddenly.

Alex wasted no time in shoving off, determined to catch up with Demetri. He could see his opponent taking a zipper line through the steep moguls, no more than twenty feet ahead of him. Unless he fell, there was little chance of catching up here. But after the mogul field would Demetri take the less steep trail that curved around to the bottom, or would he stay underneath the chair, where the terrain got rougher and there were multiple small cliffs? In the darkness, even a small drop off could be dangerous.

Alex watched as Demetri crossed over a cat track and headed underneath the lift. Alex's mind was now made up; he wouldn't lose the race by opting for the easier run down the mountain. He was pleasantly surprised to see Demetri check his speed at the end of the cat track, a critical error that would enable Alex to pass him. However, the rough terrain on this section would easily let either racer gain ground through good skiing and bravery.

Alex launched off the lip of the track onto the run, flying several feet in the air. He had already passed Demetri when he touched down, but he immediately had to slow down to regain control. As he bounced from bump to bump he began to fear that he had made a strategic error by entering the slope as quickly as he did. In the darkness, he couldn't see more than a few feet in front of him, preventing him from planning his turns in advance.

The sounds of skis scraping on snow were right behind him, and Alex knew Demetri was tailing him close. "Out of my way!" Demetri yelled in his ear. They were close enough Alex feared a collision, which could seriously injure them both here. He saw the cliff only a split second before going over it, but he moved slightly to the right to reduce the likelihood that Demetri would land on top of him.

Demetri's landing spot was steeper than Alex's, and he shot forward to be even with Alex. Seeing his rival next to him, he whipping his pole across Alex's chest and pushed him back. Alex tried to push the pole out of his way, but only managed to push himself back. Thinking quickly, he looped a finger around the pole next to the basket, and pulled Demetri quickly toward him, turning further right as he did so.

There was a satisfying grinding noise as Demetri's skis were yanked off track and hit the rock. Alex didn't look back, but he could hear the thump as Demetri hit the ground, as well as a loud scream. At that speed, hitting a rock surely meant at least one, if not both, of his skis had come off. The scream was the realization that there was no way to win at this point, and Alex would beat him to the finish line. And win Helen's heart, once and for all.

Alex slowed down, confident that Demetri wouldn't even find his skis in the dark, much less get them on, before Alex was shaking Goblin's hand.

# 12:10 AM

# The Double Black Bar and Grill

The Angry Sex Puppies were playing. And the Double Black Bar and Grill was packed.

The Angry Sex Puppies were best described, if they had to be described at all, as a psychobilly punk band. Mixing rockabilly with punk rock, they were inspired by bands such as Southern Culture on the Skids, The HorrorPops, and The Reverend Horton Heat. They had only four band members: a vocalist, a guitarist, a drummer, and a strange woman with a shaved head who played the upright double bass. An electric upright double bass, of course.

The music was fast and lively, as was their style, and as a result the bar was loud. Patrons pressed up against the stage, pushed shoulder to shoulder fifty feet deep, bouncing up and down in time with the rapid music.

The tourists had all but gone to sleep, and the

bar was crowded with the locals. Instructors, lifties, ticket sales, and even the folks who swept the cafeteria; they had all grown accustomed to the ski resort life. On weekends they would often only receive three hours of sleep, but they would make up the deficit during the slower weekdays. During the Ridge Mountain Snow Festival sleep was certainly a rare commodity.

It was less crowded near the back, and although there were no longer any empty booths, Nick was the sole occupant of the booth furthest from the stage. He wasn't a huge fan of the Angry Sex Puppies, but he did enjoy their latest hit single. They hadn't played Tripping Through the Nosegays yet, and he figured they were likely to close with it.

While he waited for his song to play, he was taking advantage of the relative peace and quiet to practice his lines. He still had no idea why his friends had run out when he showed up to the rehearsal, but they were clearly at least as drunk as he was, and who knew what they were thinking. As long as he got his lines right, it wouldn't be him making a fool of himself on the stage.

Nick took another sip of his beer and resumed his lines aloud. "But to be frank, and give it thee again. And yet I wisch but for the thing I have. My bounty is as boundlesch as the sche, my love ash deep. The more I give to thee, the more I have, for both are infinite." He was pleased with his oration.

"Thatsch very pretty," said a voice beside him. "Didsch you writesch that yourschelf?"

Nick looked at the girl who had slid into the booth beside him. She looked familiar, and he was certain she worked at the resort, but he couldn't place her face.

"Your art isch really pretty..." Anna continued, reaching up to touch his face. Nick leaned back, unsure of what to make of this new development. "Aw, don't letsch me schdop you. Go on, go on!"

Nick looked back down at his paper. "I'm practiching, for a play tomorrow."

Anna rested her chin on her fist, elbow on the table. "Go ahead, then. Scholl me."

"I hear schome noisch within. Dear love, adieu!"

"Adieu? What doesch that mean?"

"I think it meansch goodbye."

"Oh." Anna looked intently at Nick. "Go on, itsch beautiful."

"Anon, good nursch! Shweet Montague, be true."

"Isch thisch Englisch? Thisch schounds like French."

Nick considered this. "Theresch schome

French in there, like Montague."

"What doesch Montague mean in Englisch?"

"Lover, babe, scheetheart." Nick waved at his paper. "May I?"

"Oh, yesch!"

"Stay but a little, I will come again."

Anna smiled a very wicked smile. "I schure would like to make that happen!"

"Huh?"

Anna looked Nick in the eyes, and he returned the favor. "Thisch schounsch crazy, but I thinksch I lovesch you."

Nick took another large gulp of his beer and tried to decide if he heard the beautiful girl beside him correctly. He put down his glass just in time to watch her place her hand on his face.

"I lovesch you… What isch your name?"

"Nick. You?"

"Anna." With that, Anna slowly moved in and kissed him. After a brief moment, her lips parted and a tongue entered Nick's mouth. She then moved back and looked him in the eyes. "How wasch that?"

Nick couldn't remember the last time a girl kissed him, and two different girls had kissed him tonight. He silently resolved to get drunk more often. "That wasch amazching."

"Letch do it more." Anna moved closer, and they

resumed French kissing in the booth. They kissed each other in a fury of drink and drug induced lust, leaving no molar unturned in their exploration of each other's cavities. When *Tripping Through the Nosegays* started to play, Nick didn't even notice.

When Nick's hand rose up to cup Anna's breast through her shirt, however, Ron did notice. "Damn, this is good," he muttered to himself, recording the entire scene on his cellphone. "I wonder who that ass is she's with is..."

## 12:20 AM

## Outside Ridge Mountain Ski Resort Main Lodge

Most skiers are familiar with night skiing. Large lights illuminate the slopes, their bright sodium yellow lights creating a giant contrast between the white snow and the black sky. The textures of the slope cast harsh shadows on the snow, the previous day's tracks creating a crosshatch pattern of light and dark across the run. The cold night air bites at any exposed skin, keeping late-night skiers alert and awake. Night skiing is big business, with many resorts offering deeply discounted tickets to keep the slopes full well into the night.

But true night skiing is something else entirely. When the lights are off and the moon reflects off the snow. In this darkness, trees and rocks appear pitch black, holes in your vision against the dim gray snow. The sky is filled with light from the stars, and the ground is lit by the moon, but the horizon is a band of black holding it together, except where you can see sister mountains as shadows, the glow of faraway urban civilizations backlighting their scraggly peaks.

Night skiing on a resort differs in sound, as well. The night air is filled with the sounds of skiers and riders, and many resorts blast rock music from speakers mounted on light poles or lift towers. True night skiing is entirely silent. Most of the animals have put to bed, and you're high enough the sounds of the roads won't carry to your ears. It is completely and utterly silent. Combined with the pitch darkness around you, it's immensely relaxing.

Spending the night on a mountain can be a truly wonderful experience. Spending the night on a mountain because you have a broken leg can be a truly horrific one.

Helen continued to pout as Alex gave Goblin a high-five and won the race. She didn't want either one to win, and certainly not Alex. She hadn't decided what they were up to, but she didn't like it, and she absolutely didn't want to encourage it.

Still, she was worried when Alex came over to her.

"Hey, Helen, I won! Shouldn't the victor get a congratulatory kiss?"

"Go away, Alex!"

Alex put his arm around her, but she

immediately shrugged it off. "Oh, come on, don't be like that. I won fair and square!"

"There's no fair in a Chinese downhill! Where is Demetri, anyway?"

It was Alex's turn to shrug. "I don't know. He fell somewhere on Nine Ball."

"Nine Ball? In the dark? Are you insane?"

"What? It's not like I forced him down there. He took that way first; I followed him in."

"And you didn't stop to help him when he fell?"

"I had already passed him before he fell. Besides, he's a big boy, he can take care of himself. Now let's you and me go back to the Double Black and get to know each other better. I bet the Angry Sex Puppies are still playing…"

"No! Go away, you pompous ass!" Helen began marching off toward the locker room.

"Come on, Helen, don't be like that!" Alex stood forlornly watching her leave for a few minutes, then trotted off to the Double Black, hoping he would catch her in a better mood later in the night.

Helen fumed as she squeezed into her ski boots. She could hike up just as quickly without them, but she stood little chance of bringing an injured person off the mountain without skis. She just hoped she could handle bringing Demetri down alone, assuming that she could find him in the first place.

Barely five minutes had passed since she left

the snow, and her second largest fear was that Demetri had come down during that time. Her biggest fear was that he hadn't. Strapping her skis onto her backpack and grabbing her poles, Helen set off up the slope.

It was only a few minutes hike before Nine Ball Run became steep and ungroomed, and she debated taking an easier run up. But she had no idea how high up the mountain Demetri had been lost, and didn't want to risk missing him and forcing him to spend the night alone in the cold. She turned on her climbing headlamp and trudged through the snow, calling his name out every few minutes.

Fortunately, she did not have to climb to the top before hearing a response to her cries. She quickly found Demetri, huddled in a ball under an overhang, shivering from the cold. She quickly shed her jacket and placed it over him.

"My God, Demetri, are you alright?"

"My leg... I think my right leg is broken."

Helen gingerly felt the leg through his pants, ignoring his suppressed gasps and whimpers as best she could. "It doesn't feel like compound fracture; is there any blood?"

"I don't think so, I can't feel any."

"Can you feel all your fingers and toes?"

"Yeah, but they're cold. They sting a little."

"That's good. That means they still have blood flowing through them."

Demetri regained some of his composure just knowing he was going to be alright. "Where did you learn all this?"

"I started by teaching first aid at the YWCA, but the last two years I've done volunteer mountain search and rescue."

"Really?" Demetri was genuinely impressed. "I didn't know that. Am I going to be okay?"

Helen laughed. "Oh, you'll be okay. You may not ski again this winter, but you'll be fine by next season. I'm going to have to get you down, though. Where are your skis?"

"I'm not sure. I fell down about twenty feet up; my guess is they're in the woods not too far from here."

"Which side?"

Demetri reconstructed the accident in his head. "Probably the right side."

"Great. You stay put, okay?" Helen dropped her backpack and took off into the trees. She reappeared a few minutes later carrying Demetri's skis back to him.

"I can't ski down, Helen!"

"You're not going to. I'm going to build a sled, and you're going to ride down."

"You've got to be kidding me, right? Have you done this before?"

"Sorta." Helen was pulling ropes out of her

backpack. "Hand me your poles, would you?"

"What do you mean, sorta?"

"I did it with dummies. With real victims we always let the bigger guys do it; it's hard to control a heavy sled."

The good feeling that came with knowing he would be taken care of vanished as quickly as it arrived. "Maybe we should call someone else?"

Helen tightened the knot she was working on, inspected her work. "Nope, it would take at least an hour, probably longer, before anyone got up here. I need to get you to warmth now. Now come on, you big baby, it's time to get on the sled."

The ride down was rough, and Demetri's leg flared in pain with each bump. Still, it was certainly better than spending the night alone on the mountainside. The ride also gave him time to think about Helen, and how kind she was being to him after the way he had treated her. Would he have done the same if she were lost on the mountain, or would he have just reported her missing and gone on with his night? She certainly was a special woman.

# 12:45 AM

# The Double Black Bar and Grill

It began to snow again. Late night snow was heaven for the early riser hitting the slopes as the rope first dropped. Fresh powder, without time to compress and stiffen, allows the skier to fly through it without ever touching a firm surface. It is every skier's dream.

The groomers, on the other hand, do not like it. While most of the resort is asleep, or in a few cases still partying hard, the groomers are responsible for packing down the snow on the beginner and intermediate slopes to ensure the consistent corduroy surface that is easy to ride on. This job takes many hours, and requires an early morning start. It's certainly not easy to accomplish while it is still snowing on you, as early work can be erased before opening and require a second run.

The groomers may be the most underappreciated workers at the entire ski resort. Many of the customers come and go without even thinking about them once. The beginners may not even realize that the snow they ski on has been groomed to make it easier to learn, and advanced skiers may complain about groomers taking the fun out of slopes by making them too easy. But even they need grooming to make the crowded base areas navigable, and few of them would even think to spend these early morning hours riding a large cat up and down the mountain.

Nobody in the Double Black Bar and Grill was thinking of the groomers right now. The Angry Sex Puppies had just walked off the stage, and then returned triumphantly to play *Tripping Through the Nosegays* one last time before quitting for good. The crowd was euphoric, not to mention drunk, and the bar was yet to close for some time.

Alex had returned in time to catch *Tripping Through the Nosegays* and nothing else, and now he considered what to do next. He didn't understand why Helen had rebuffed him after winning the race, but it was starting to become more clear. Did he really dump Mia for Helen over an instantaneous crush? How much had he been drinking? What on earth had he done?

Alex wandered through the bar, looking for Mia. He hadn't seen her since he agreed to compete in that stupid race, but as far as he could tell she hadn't come to the slopes with the others. He briefly considered texting her, but realized there would be no point. She wouldn't answer his texts, or even read them. Why should she?

Eventually he found her standing alone in a corner, nursing a beer. He walked up beside her. "Mia," he said softly.

"Go away."

"I want to talk to you."

"I said go away."

"I just wanted to say I was sorry." Alex was glad the band had stopped playing; he didn't want to have to yell this out.

"Go away, or I'm leaving."

"Please, Mia? Just let me talk."

Mia stood silently, but didn't leave.

"Look, I don't know what happened to me. I guess I was drunk or something, and I acted a right ass."

"Yes, you were."

Mia had said something other than "go away." Alex considered this an improvement. "Look, I love you. I have for a long time. I don't know why I was acting so dumb, but I don't want to throw away everything we've built together over some stupid night."

"You should have thought of that before you started chasing that harlot."

Alex smirked. Helen was hardly a harlot. "We've had a lot of good times together, and I love you a lot.

Do you still love me?"

Mia looked Alex in the eyes for the first time during this conversation. "Yeah, I guess I do."

"Then let's not throw this all away! Mia, I love you. I want to marry you!"

Mia stifled a laugh. "You've hardly been acting it tonight!"

"You're right, I haven't. But I will from now on."

"Promise?"

Alex took Mia's hand into his own. "I promise, Mia. I'll be faithful to you forever more."

Mia smiled softly. As hurt as she was, it still felt good to hear Alex's words.

"Come on, let me buy you a beer?"

"I think you've had more than enough for tonight, Alex. Go home. I'll see you in the morning, okay?"

Alex looked down. "Yeah, you're right. I'll see you in the locker room then?"

"Yeah."

"And we're cool?"

"Well, let's just say I'll be expecting a really nice Christmas present this year."

Alex leaned in and gave Mia a quick peck on the lips. Pulling away, he reconsidered and moved back in for a more passionate kiss. She raised a finger to his lips, halting his progress. "One step at a time, boy. Go get yourself some sleep."

# 1:30 AM

# Ski Patrol Shack

Few things cure a hangover better than a broken bone. If anything is better, it would be the feeling of flying down a slope, with the cold wind whipping at your cheeks and snowflakes rushing into your lungs.

A daily ritual for many skiers involves rolling out of bed at the crack of dawn, haphazardly pulling on pants, pouring a cup of coffee and staggering out into the cold. Hung over, and possibly still drunk from the night before, they'll wander up the streets toward the resort. A few may pause to dry heave over a planter or sewer grating. Finally, the rope will drop and the fuzzy-headed skiers will load the chairlift, reluctantly pulled against the force of gravity to the top of the mountain.

As they tighten their bindings, they collectively have an entire fleet of furry lobsters laying within their skulls. But the moment when they hear the sound of the skis sliding over the snow, the feel of the cold air whipping through the hair, and the weightlessness that happens as they drop over the cornice lip, the stomach falls into line and the electrolyte levels magically stabilize. It's almost as if the brain tells the body, "Your time to be sick is past; now it is time to ski."

If skiing is the best hangover cure, a broken bone is the second best, scoring higher than a jalapeño coffee chaser. And right now Demetri was not feeling the effects of the alcohol, or even the drugs, any more. Instead, Demetri was feeling the pain in his right leg.

"Hold still, this is going to sting," said the ski patroller, as he jabbed a needle into Demetri's leg.

"Sting? My leg is burning! The needle is nothing!"

"Well, this will help with that. You're lucky I stayed around for the show at the Double Black; I'll have this set in a jiffy." All the ski patrollers had medical training, but only a few were actual doctors. There were a few weekend volunteer doctors, as well as a few retired doctors who decided to spend their retirement on the snow. Helen had been lucky enough to find Dr. Steve Goodman still wearing his jacket at the Double Black. "What were you doing up on the mountain so late?"

"Skiing."

Dr. Goodman shrugged as he began wrapping the leg. "Not very well, it seems."

"Well, it was dark."

"And you were drunk."

Demetri would have shifted uncomfortably, but he couldn't shift through the pain, and even just sitting still was uncomfortable. So he just sat still, uncomfortably.

Helen cleared her throat from around the corner. "Are you decent?"

"Yeah, come on in." Helen did.

"How's it look?"

The doctor put the final wraps on the leg. "He'll need to get a proper cast in the morning, after some x-rays. But as far as I can tell from here, it looks like a clean break. I'd wager that as long as he doesn't put any pressure on it before the cast is on, he should be skiing again in six to eight weeks. He's very lucky that you were there to rescue him."

Helen looked down at Demetri. "How am I going to get you out of here?"

The patroller looked at the clock on the wall. "Technically, nobody is allowed to be in here at night. But you're both employees, and it's practically morning anyway. I'll send the boss a text, and Demetri can spend the night here."

Helen looked up from the aching instructor. "Thanks, that will be great."

Demetri pushed himself up onto his elbows. "Could you stay here with me? I know it's almost morning anyway, but this really does hurt and I'd hate to be alone."

Helen looked at the patroller. "Would that be okay?"

"Sure, I guess. I'll grab some more blankets and pillows, and you can grab any bunk."

"Thanks."

Dr. Goodman finished the splint, and inspected his work in silence. Finally, he stood up. "Well, that's all I can do tonight. Remember to get him to a hospital in the morning."

Demetri extended his hand. "Thanks, doc."

They shook. "Don't worry about it. But next time you get yourself drunk late at night, don't go out for a midnight run, okay?"

"You got it, doc."

Dr. Goodman grabbed his jacket and backpack and headed out the door. "I'll see you two in the morning. We usually start arriving around seven, so get some sleep while you can." He locked the door behind himself as he left.

Helen stood next to Demetri for a few uncomfortable moments, then moved to make her bunk. "Stay with me for a few minutes, please?" pleaded Demetri. "I'm not going to be able to fall asleep for a while. This still really hurts."

"Um, okay." Helen sat down on Demetri's bunk, causing him to wince. "Oh, sorry! Did that hurt?"

"Just a little. Don't worry, it'll be okay." The two sat in silence for a few more moments, then Demetri spoke again. "So... Why did you come for me? I mean, after the way I'd been treating you?"

Helen snorted dismissively. "I'd rescue anyone on the mountain. It's not right to leave anyone up there where they could freeze to death."

"Yeah, but I've been a right ass to you."

"Yes, you have. But a broken leg is punishment enough; you shouldn't have to die, too."

"Does this mean I'm forgiven?"

Helen laughed. "No, it means you've been punished. Forgiveness takes time." She turned her head and looked at Demetri's crestfallen expression, then looked into his eyes for the first time since coming into the shack. "Oh, hell. Yes, I forgive you."

"Thanks. You're a good woman. I regret everything I've said about you in the past."

"Well, that might take a little longer to forgive. But you're making a good start." Helen stood up to go to bed, but stopped when she was next to Demetri's head. Spontaneously, she leaned over and gave him a quick peck on the forehead, as her mother had done to her when she had a fever. Her lips lingered on Demetri's skin a little longer than her mother's had. When she finished, she remained bent over, hovering above his face, acutely aware of what she had just done. "I'm sorry," she whispered.

"Don't be." Demetri turned his head up to look her in the eye, and propping himself on his elbows, he kissed her chastely on the lips.

"Oh, shit," bemoaned Helen. "You're not going start saying you love me more than anything again, are you?"

"No, I don't know what made me say that. But you are a wonderful woman, and I'd like to get to know you better. After the doctors put me back together, can I take you out to see a movie or something?"

"Yeah, I'd like that." Helen paused, then leaned down to give him one more kiss on the lips. This time the contact was less chaste, and her lips parted to allow his invading tongue access. She hadn't been kissed like this in a long time, and it ignited a hunger inside her. She ran her hands down his chest, pulling herself deeper into him.

Demetri's hands responded by roaming up Helen's back, initially over her shirt, but as the kiss progressed they slipped under the fabric. When they started fiddling with her bra strap, Helen pulled herself upright.

"We shouldn't be doing this," she gasped.

"Why not?"

"First, it's late."

"I'm not sleepy."

"Second, your leg is broken."

"I can deal with that."

"Third..." Helen paused. "Damn it, I had a third reason!"

"Come here."

"Shit," muttered Helen as she came back to the rack. She carefully swung her leg over Demetri and straddled him. He winced but didn't complain as she settled down. "Well, here goes nothing," she said, as she pulled her shirt up and over her head.

# 6:30 AM

# Lift Attendant Locker Room

Caffeine.

Caffeine stands as humanity's most widely used drug, edging out tobacco and alcohol. It's one of a few number of psychoactive drugs available without a prescription, and millions of people self-administer it on a daily basis. Globally, the planet averages one caffeinated beverage, per person, per day.

Nobody knows when humans first starting using caffeine. There is a legend that five thousand years ago, Chinese emperor Shennong discovered that when tea leaves were placed into boiling water, it produced a drink that would refresh and rejuvenate the drinker. However, evidence suggests that Native Americans were consuming a caffeinated tea made from a holly plant thousands of years before the Chinese.

Today caffeine is available not only as tea, but in sodas, chocolate, and pill form. One company even sells caffeinated water, which can be used in creating a caffeine-infused version of the buyer's favorite beverage. However, the majority of caffeine consumed is found within a single beverage – coffee.

There's a myth that caffeine doesn't work at high altitudes. While nobody knows who started this myth, it certainly wasn't a skier. Or a lift attendant. Lift attendants live by coffee.

This morning, Peter was barely living by his. From the look on the faces of the lift attendants huddled around, coffee was the only thing keeping them alive.

"Alright, roll call. Who's here?" There were no responses. "Come on, lads, who's here this morning?"

"Fuck you, Peter," someone volunteered from the back.

"If you're going to be like that, we'll go down the list one at a time. Frank?"

"Hung over," Frank moaned.

"You should drink less. Get yourself a cup of coffee." Frank did.

"Tom?" Peter glared at Tom, waiting for a response. "Tom?" The lack of response remained, so Peter tapped his pen against his clipboard meaningfully. "TOM!"

Tom looked up from his insulated mug. "Feel like shit, Peter."

Peter tapped his pen several times against

his clipboard, in the apparent hopes that it would convey the seriousness of the situation, or at a bare minimum, wake the lifties up. "What the hell did you guys do last night?" he finally exclaimed.

"Buggered to a tee if I know."

"Fuck, I don't remember."

"Couldn't tell you if my next two paychecks depended on it."

"Peter," Nick interjected. "Please allow me to set the scene." He placed his insulated coffee mug down on the table in front of him, and stood up. "It was a night of merriment, and a night for imbibing great quantities of spirits. A night of music, a night of magic, and a night of love." He paused, remembering a few moments that Anna would probably prefer he forgot. "It was a night of human wonder, and truly a night beyond the wit of man."

"That's nice, Nick. Real nice. Can we please get on with the meeting now?"

Nick sat down and picked up his mug. He took a slow sip and set it back down. If he had accomplished nothing else, he had at least prevented Peter from taking another muster. "Sure, why not?"

"Listen, Peter, we have to talk about the play. We're performing it this morning, and Frank's not letting me add any new lines to his part!"

"Why would we add lines to his part?"

"Because I'm supposed to be a talking dog, and

if I talk but he doesn't answer, I'm going to look like a really stupid dog!"

"You are a stupid dog, Robin!" Robin threw a wadded piece of paper at Frank.

Peter tried to regain control of the meeting. "Look, Frank, have you memorized the lines Robin wrote?"

"Hell, no!"

"Well, then, that settles it. It's far too late to go changing the play. Everyone will say the lines that they've been practicing."

"But that's... stupid!" shouted Robin.

The entire group had caught on by this point. "But you are a stupid dog, Robin!" they shouted in unison.

Peter looked at the yellow sticky note which contained the topics he actually wanted to talk about today, along with an inspirational quote. Once again the moisture had reduced it to splotches and smears.

"Look, men, when you're out there bumping chairs, I want you to remember the words of Shakespeare when he said," Peter squinted, "To the one shelf be blue."

Silence echoed through the room.

"What the hell does that mean?" asked Nick.

Peter sighed. "Just go and do your damn jobs."

# 7:30 AM

# Snow Sports School Locker Room

It may seem ironic to some that the top reason that ski instructors get fired is for skiing. By some strange coincidence, every time a deep layer of soft new snow appears, the same group of instructors seems to come down with the flu. When a holiday weekend where the instructors all know they'll be working all day without a moment to enjoy the conditions themselves happens to coincide with fresh snow, even the most honest instructors feel a tinge of a sore throat.

Resorts can prevent a lot of this by disabling sick employee's passes for the day, but that only helps a little. More creative employees will drive to neighboring resorts and buy passes with cash, ensuring a work-free day of skiing. In the end, the only surefire way to catch these malingerers is to keep track of sick days, and fire the instructors who seem to have allergies to busy days and fresh snow. Ridge Mountain did this well, and nobody who faked illness could expect to finish out the season. As a result, all the instructors braved snow, wind, cold, and hangovers to be at the morning meeting on time.

Today was going to be a very busy day. The climax of the Ridge Mountain Snow Festival was often its busiest day of the year, and this year it coincided with fresh power. But nobody even thought of calling in today with the flu; today, hangovers predominated. If there's one thing a ski school supervisor can recognize, it's an instructor with a hangover pretending to be sick. So everyone was present for the morning meeting.

Ron leaned against the side of a locker. The morning meeting had just ended, and he needed to get outside to cruise a few slopes and get his adrenaline running so that he could put the lingering effects of the night before behind him. First, however, he needed to pee, and he would have to wait until the restroom was available to do that.

"'SUP DAWG!" shouted Goblin, immediately behind him. Ron groaned.

"Damn, why'd you do a thing like that? Shit, you know how late we were out last night."

"Yeah, I was with you, remember?" Goblin's ability to survive a night without sleep and enough alcohol to embalm an elephant was legendary. The joy he had at the expense of others less fortunate was also well known. "Let's go get some pow before the first classes!"

"Yeah, yeah, I gotta pee first. Helen's in there."

"Whatever, dude." Goblin smiled. "You got the board yet?"

"Shit, no, I haven't even thought about it. Haven't talked to Anne at all; you seen her?"

"Yeah, she was in the meeting. Sitting in the back, quiet like."

"Good. Hopefully she remembers what happened... But if she doesn't, I've got video."

"You scoundrel!" Goblin donned his gloves. "You heading out for some pow?"

"In a sec, I gotta use the pisser."

"Whatever. No friends on a powder day, eh? I'll see you around the mountain, loser." With that, Goblin walked off towards the door.

The door opened and Helen walked out. "Oh, hey, Ron. I guess you're next."

"Yeah," he responded, walking in.

Helen spotted Mia closing her locker nearby. "Mia, we need to talk."

Mia turned to face Helen. "Look, Helen, I'm sorry about last night. I'd been drinking, and I didn't understand what was going on. Hell, I still don't understand what happened, but I talked to Alex, and I think we're okay."

"Mia, I just wanted to apologize for-"

"No, you didn't do anything wrong. I'm the one who needs to apologize."

Helen gave Mia a quick hug. "It's good, girl." She paused as she stepped back. "Hey, want to go for a run?"

"Nah, I need to take care of a few things first. I'll be out soon."

"Okay, no problem. I'll see you out there."

"Wait, Helen, what happened to you last night? I didn't see you after that stupid race."

"I went up and rescued Demetri. He broke his leg."

"Seriously? Oh my God, is he alright?"

"Yeah, out for the season, but I don't think it will be anything more serious. He's at the hospital now, getting x-rayed."

"He's lucky that you're such a wonderful person. After the way he treated you, anyone else would have left him up there. And he probably doesn't even realize it, either."

"I think he does. We talked a bunch, and I think we're a lot closer now."

"He apologized?"

"I suppose you could say that."

Mia looked at Helen confused. Realization dawned on her. "You didn't!" Helen blushed. "Oh my God, you DID! I can't believe that!"

"Twice."

"Helen!"

"I know, I know. But wow. Just WOW."

Mia giggled. "Well, someone had a good night last night! Where were you two?"

"In the ski patrol shack."

"You dirty little slut! Wow."

Helen waved off Mia's admiration. "And you and Alex are good now?"

Mia shrugged. "I think we're okay. He's in the doghouse, though."

"Who is?" Alex appeared behind Mia, surprising her. "I got you something."

Mia turned around to see Alex's head poking through a large bundle of flowers. She laughed. "For me?"

"Of course, dear."

Helen picked up her skis. "I'll just be seeing myself out, then."

"Don't think this means you're completely out of trouble, mister." Mia took the flowers and placed them in her locker. "It will take more than flowers to make up for all the crap you pulled."

"Would a kiss help?" Alex leaned in for a kiss, and this time, Mia didn't stop him.

The door opened, and Ron stepped out. "Damn, girls, get a room." Mia just laughed. "Well, it looks like you two are still together."

Alex gave her another kiss, this one chaste. "Always and forever."

"Ugh, I'm going to puke. See you two lovebirds out on the snow."

Ron walked to his locker to retrieve his snowboard. When he got there, he found Anna was waiting for him, eyes downcast. "Hey Ron."

Ron smiled. "What's up girl?"

"I was just thinking. I really love you, Ron."

"I love you too, babycakes.... Is there something you're trying to tell me?"

"No, no..." Anne hesitated. "Well, maybe sorta. I mean, I want you to know that I love you a lot, but sometimes even though someone loves someone a lot, they still make mistakes, you know?"

"No, babe, I don't know what you're talking about."

"Look, I got drunk last night and did something stupid. I don't want you to think that I love you any less because of it. We all make mistakes, you know?"

"You mean like falling down because you're on a snowboard that's too big and stiff for you?"

Anna sighed. "Yeah, like that."

Ron put his arm around Anna. He was hoping that he wouldn't have to show her the video, if only because she would be likely to punch him. "Well, whatever you did, I'm sure it's not that bad. I'm sure you could think of a way to make it up to me. What did you do, anyway?"

Anne returned her gaze to the ground. "I kinda made out with someone else."

Ron feigned shock. "What? With who?"

"I don't remember, to be honest. I was pretty drunk."

"Did you enjoy it?"

"Kinda. He was an animal."

Ron shook his head. "Babe, I don't know about that. If you really loved me, you wouldn't be kissing other guys."

Anna pulled Ron in for a hug. "Please, baby, forgive me! It was the alcohol talking, I swear!"

"I don't know." Ron pushed her away. "That's pretty serious."

Anna paused again. "What if... What if I gave you my snowboard? Would that prove that I really love you?"

This time Ron pulled Anna in for a hug, if only so she couldn't see him smile in victory. "Yeah, baby, that might do it."

Meanwhile Mia walked into George's office, grabbing a sports drink as she did. "Morning, Dad."

George looked up from the schedule he was working on. "Morning. Mia. I was hoping to have a chance to talk to you this morning."

Mia slumped down into a chair. She wasn't looking forward to yet another lecture from her father.

"Look, Mia, you're the most important person in my life, and I want what's best for you. Sometimes what you want and what's best for you aren't the same thing." Mia sighed and sipped from her drink. "I know you want to be with Alex, but I think Demetri could provide for you better."

"Dad, I don't want to go over this again. I'm not going to marry Demetri. For one, I don't love him. For two, he-"

George cut her off. "Just listen to me, Mia. I was raised in a different culture than you. When I was a child, parents would arrange their children's lives to help them out. Here, today, children are expected to make their own mistakes."

Mia started to speak again, but George cut her off again. "I still believe that in the long run you'd be happier with Demetri. But I realize now that it's not my choice to make. If you want to stay with Alex, then that's your choice."

"Dad, I'm trying to tell you- Wait, wait?"

"I said you have my blessing to date Alex."

Mia jumped up and ran around the desk to hug her father. "Thank you!"

George shrugged her off. "Alright, alright, sit down and act like a lady."

Mia grabbed her sports drink. "You know what my second reason was?"

"No, what was it?"

"Demetri's dating Helen now."

George dropped his pen. "That cheeky bastard!"

## 10:30 AM
## Ridge Mountain Ski Resort
## Main Stage

It's a miracle that the works of William Shakespeare are still performed today. There are many playwrights and poets of the era whose plays are still performed today, yet outside of select intellectual circles are virtually unknown. Why haven't John Fletcher, Francis Beaumont, Christopher Marlowe, Thomas Kyd, or Ben Johnson received the same household name status as William Shakespeare? Two hundred years from now, will Steven King be a household name while J.K. Rowling withers into obscurity, or the other way around?

The fact is most Shakespeare plays don't even translate well to a modern audience. *Romeo and Juliet* is just a depressing story of how bigotry and anger cannot be overcome by love, and it's riddled with plot holes. Even the comedies can be depressing, as a *Midsummer Night's Dream* can demonstrate. What moral is taught by Oberon, the King of the Fairies, who commands Puck to use magic to trick Titania and force her to hand over a young Indian prince to him. He suffers no consequences for his evil plan. To Elizabethan audiences, he was a king who got his way, and they saw nothing wrong with it. But what modern audience wouldn't prefer to see Oberon get his comeuppance by having his plan backfire on him?

What sets Shakespeare apart from his contemporaries is, of course, his outstanding wordplay. The wit of his prose, and the puns sprinkled liberally throughout all his works, stand head and shoulders above the works of others. Unfortunately, as language evolves, many of those also fall flat on the ears of anyone unschooled in Elizabethan culture and language.

For an example, look to Mercutio and Romeo meeting the nurse. Mercutio hollars "A bawd! A bawd! A bawd! So ho!", to which Romeo replies "What hast thou found?". Mercutio answers "No hare, sir, unless, sir, a hare in a lenten pie, that is something stale and hoar ere it be spent." Does that make sense to the average American? I think not.

Perhaps if you knew that bawd, hare, stale, and whore all meant a prostitute at the time, and hoar meant white, and also that a lenten pie was eaten slowly through lent so that it would be stale and white (hoar) before being spent (eaten completely), then one might be able to comprehend the complexity of this pun. But to the average viewer watching Leonardo DeCaprio play Romeo on their television, it's a line that simply makes no sense.

So what of Shakespeare? Should we cease performing these awesome works because we no longer understand them? Of course not! Rather, we perform them, and every now and then we grasp a play on words, and having grasped on, we get a momentary glimpse of how great the works truly were in their heyday.

But today the Ridge Mountain Snow Festival was going to be treated to a rendition of the balcony scene that would not serve such a purpose. Hastily constructed cardboard scenery adorned the stage that had hosted the Angry Sex Puppies the night before, while various departments presented skits and other amusements.

Phil walked onto the stage with his microphone, thanking the groomers for their performance. "And now, ladies and gentlemen, for your viewing pleasure... The Ridge Mountain Ski Resort Lift Operations Department presents..." Phil glanced at his notecard, "The balcony scene from William Shakespeare's *Romeo and Juliet*!" There were a few polite claps from the assembled audience.

A cardboard sheet painted to look like a balcony was placed on one side of the stage, and a cardboard sheet painted to look like a bush was placed in the center. Frank walked to the center of the stage, while

Robin trotted on all fours behind him.

"Psst! Frank! They can't see me behind this cardboard bush!"

"Shut up, Robin, we're starting!"

"Frank! I'll not hide behind a bush!"

"I'll hide you, Robin! Keep quiet!" Frank raised his voice and shouted "He jests at scars that never felt a wound!" Hearing his cue, Nick walked onto the stage and stood behind the cardboard balcony. "But soft, what light through wonder window breaks? It is the West, and Juliet is the sun. Arise, fair sun, and kill the envious moon, who is already sick and pale with grief, that thou are made far more fair than she. Be not made, but be envious; her vestigial liver is but sick and green; cast it off. It is my lady, O, it is my love! O, that she knew she were! She speaks yet she says nothing: what of that?"

"**ARF**!" barked Robin, who had walked in front of the bush during Frank's travesty of recitation.

Frank nodded at Robin and continued. "Aye, discourse; I will answer it. I am too bold, 'tis not to me she speaks: two of the fairest stars in all the heaven, having some business, do entreat her eyes to twinkle in their spheres till they return. What if her eyes were not there in her head? The brightness of her cheek would shame those stars, as daylight doth a lamp; her eyes in heaven would through the airy region stream so bright that birds would sing and think it were not night. See, how she leans her cheek upon her hand! O, that I were a glove upon that hand, that I might touch that cheek!"

On hearing this, Nick quickly touched his hand to his face. There was a pause of several seconds before Frank pointedly repeated "THAT I MIGHT TOUCH THAT CHEEK!"

"Oh, right," said Nick. "I, me."

Frank glared at Nick. "What the hell is wrong with you?"

"Sorry, Frank, I had a rough night. A night beyond the wit of man!"

"This fucking blows," shouted Goblin from the audience. "This will touch your cheek!" He launched a snowball at Nick that hit him square in the jaw, lodging snow in his mustache.

"You cheeky bastard!" Frank exclaimed. Robin contributed an additional bark for emphasis.

Phil ran onto the stage to attempt to salvage the show, but Theo and Lita entered from the other side, and after a quick wave, Phil handed the microphone over to Theo.

"Well, thank you for that, um, unusual rendition of *Romeo and Juliet*!"

Frank was taken aback. "We've got more!"

Theo smiled. "I'm sure you do, but what you've already performed was a dream."

"A bad dream," heckled Goblin. "You might say this entire performance has been a nightmare, even!"

Theo chuckled at the strange-haired fellow in the crowd. "Well, every day I come to this resort and see new snow on the ground is a dream. Don't you think so?" There was a loud roar of approval from the assembled crowd. "So without further ado, I'd like to remind everyone there is fresh snow on the mountain. We'll have bluegrass playing on the second stage all afternoon, and races on Lightning starting at one. So come, friends, let us put our hands together for everyone performing here on the stage today!"

Goblin began moving out of the crowd as everyone clapped. "Buggerit, I'm going riding."

Also by Jimmy Brokaw

During the fall of 2002, tens of thousands of American troops were stationed in Kuwait and Saudi Arabia, waiting for a war nobody was sure would come at all. This is the story of one such soldier. Specialist Hoffman is crazy, and he knows it. But that's not enough to get him out of the desert. His roommate extended his orders because he enjoys the extra combat pay. His other roommate is an aircraft mechanic, assigned to a tank maintenance facility due to an ancient clerical error. Together, the three experience some hilarious adventures while waiting for war.

www.ingramcontent.com/pod-product-compliance
Lightning Source LLC
Chambersburg PA
CBHW060143130626
46556CB00006B/2471